Rendered

TimeWorm Series—Book 3

TimeWorm
Vigilatus
Rendered

Journey through the passages of time.

Brenda Heller

Brenda Heller

Copyright © 2020 Brenda Heller
All rights reserved
First Edition

PAGE PUBLISHING, INC.
Conneaut Lake, PA

First originally published by Page Publishing 2020

ISBN 978-1-6624-1376-6 (pbk)
ISBN 978-1-6624-1377-3 (digital)

Printed in the United States of America

Rendered:
Surrendered, relinquished; yielded; provided as due reward

To all who learn to stand against wrong.
To all who find right in the future.

Part I
America, 1937

Request

THE CABIN DOOR BURST OPEN as a gust of wind blew in a man wearing a raccoon coat that smelled as if it smoldered from a stray ash. Gustav Kaercher kicked at the dust on the wooden floor as he crossed the room.

"Really, Gustav! Must you always make such a grand entrance! You smell like that raccoon you're wearing died along the side of the road." Fritz Kuhn sucked in a long draw from his cigarette before squashing the ashes in the glass ashtray. He gave a sideways grin and tipped back his head. "It's summer, Gustav. Take off that coat and tell me how your work goes. Are you here to trade your life of designing power plants for a life of commanding tomorrow's minions of the führer?" Again he paused with a gesture for the visitor to sit down. "Whatever the cause of your visit, it's good to see you. How is life back on German soil? Is Hitler growing jealous? Maybe his *Hitlerjugend* can't compare to the youths we train in the American bund. Does he fear being second best?"

An expressionless face stared back at the German-born American citizen. "Go ahead. Congratulate yourself on your success of brainwashing Americans at your summer camps then rubbing them in the face of the führer." Gustav Kaercher tossed the raccoon coat across a small table and collapsed onto a chair. "To answer your curiosity—if indeed you really want to know—I'm following some kids." He tipped his head as if his frown pulled his forehead down. "And I'm studying a location once used by Thomas Edison. American guilt has replaced an abandoned building with a memorial tower, but it's relatively isolated. It's my understanding that Edison always had a project or two—or ten—going at once. He was so wrapped up in his science that people ignored him. His old lab was at Menlo Park.

Besides Nikola Tesla, no one cared. Tesla's in California and Edison's dead. It will be a perfect location that will draw no suspicion."

"Interesting." Fritz Kuhn's comment was lost in insincerity and the squeak of his chair spring as he leaned back, stretching his arms to the ceiling. "You really think you can hide in plain sight?"

Undaunted, Kaercher kicked his feet up to rest on a side table. "Perhaps. If not, Edison dug an abandoned copper mine at the same Menlo Park location. Not many spelunkers hang around where there's nothing but rural dirt."

He grinned and lit a cigarette. "Don't mind if I do. Thanks for the offer, Kuhn." Gustav tipped his head as he took a drag on the cigarette to volley the spiritless conversation back to his friend.

"So how did you find this out-of-the-way abandoned building, whadya call it?"

"Menlo Park? I was told by America's boy"—Gustav Kaercher grinned as if a secret was about to be exposed—"and the führer's pet, Henry Ford."

Chuckles billowed from both men as cigarette smoke rose between them.

"What? You've turned scientist and Ford's best friend overnight? Why do you need such secret place? What underhanded project brought you back to America? Aren't you still a pawn of Viktor Brack?"

"Pawn!" Gustav nearly shouted back at Fritz. "If not for my jaunting back and forth across the waters and countryside with a journal of notes for his experiments, I'm afraid the scientific suggestions he proposes to taunt the führer would be nothing but vapors in a madman's daydreams."

"So what cryptic notes have you passed to the mad scientist?" Fritz Kuhn leaned forward with true interest.

"For starters, I've rubbed shoulders with Nikola Tesla enough to copy notes concerning x-rays."

"X-rays?" The uniformed listener sat back in his chair. "Do you tell me Viktor Brack cares for people's health? I don't believe it. He wouldn't heal the führer himself unless it meant a step up on the Reich's ladder of power."

A boisterous laugh came uncontrolled from the darkened heart of his friend. "*Nein*! Viktor Brack is a friend to no one but himself. No, no. He has suggested a concentrated form of Tesla's x-rays to control the population of Jews, you know, *medical castration*. No victim would be the wiser until weeks after the x-ray."

"Hmmm. Control of the masses that Hitler despises. And the führer's thoughts?"

Another cigarette was pressed into the ashtray. "He doesn't like it. Too slow." Kaercher blew out a last puff of smoke that had been held at the back of his throat. "But don't worry, my friend. Brack's all wrapped up in another program given the code name of T4."

"Another program? To control?"

"Ha! Control Hitler and annihilate Jews." Kaercher's voice sounded pleased, but his countenance showed stress. "That's not the reason I'm here, though. I've got too many irons in the fire. I'm hoping some of your summer minions can help me."

"Summer minions? Boys from my bund camps?" A half frown joined Kuhn's raised eyebrows.

"Think of this as extended training, my friend." Gustav sat forward as if he had suddenly become interested in his own proposal. "I need help."

"You? Need help? Since when did you ever tell anyone but your stinky jaegers that you wanted help?"

"Mental work and legwork are no challenge, Fritz; you know that, but I'm too old for my scheme." He noticed an upturn to his friend's scowl. "I need to track some kids. You have enough youth at your summer bund camps. Give them a real challenge instead of summer games. It'll help me, and you'll look good."

"Games? Is that what you think, Gustav? Marches, boxing, shooting rifles—ah, these may look like games, but watch the faces, my friend. It's not just the body we're training but also the heart. By the end of camp their salutes to Hitler and the flag cause their own parents to have nightmares of sleeping in the same house with them." He caught his throat constricting from an internal anger beginning to build. "Nonetheless, what do you propose for the boys of my camps?"

"I came tracking two teens. It seems Viktor Brack has the mental capacity to create and use science, but he failed at keeping the book of notes where I helped him write plans and formulas."

"And you think teens have your book of notes?" Now it was Kuhn's turn to laugh. "Robbed by teenagers? How? Why? Half of the kids at the bund camps are extensions of their parents' loyalty to Hitler. Maybe the kids you're tracking are decoys. Are you certain you're after the right thieves?"

"Sure of it. A jaeger caught them in the act, but they had help escaping with the book."

"What have you done? Genetically weakened a jaeger? How could a teen—or even an entire bund camp of teens—escape the grips of one of those beasts?" Fritz Kuhn shook his head in disbelief.

"They had help. Seems their guardian happened to be one of the strong arms—mentally and physically—of *The Watch*." Gustav paused to light another cigarette. "Long story short, I tracked the kids on a flight to America on the *Hindenburg*. They're in America alone. I just need a few of your boys to help locate them. I'm a little too old to play the part of a false friend."

"The *Hindenburg*!" Fritz Kuhn leaned forward and whistled. "I heard about the fiery crash. How'd you survive? No wonder that raccoon smells like a burned animal! Didn't the kids notice you on the flight?" Kuhn didn't have to feign interest.

"I'm smart enough to know that my jump from the *Hindenburg* would be more important to me than chasing teenagers through the flames. I had a *Hitlerjugend* with me on the flight. He worked as a cabin boy and reported back to me. Unfortunately, he didn't survive the crash. So, I'm here looking for more teens who can help me get near the kids." A puff of smoke drifted from Kaercher's pursed lips to hang in the air of the cabin.

"I see. Well, you've come to the right place. This is worthy training ground. I'll secretly train a few before we send them on your mission. Come to a camp and watch for a few days. Then pick who you think will work best to help you track these boys."

"Good. You understand my need. I'll take you up on your offer, but there's something else you need to know." A crooked grin spread from the corner of the lips that pinched a cigarette. "Not two boys. One's a girl."

Gustav Kaercher walked into the sunshine, satisfied as he slammed the door of a new red Ford coupe and drove back toward Raritan Township. "Thanks for the car, Henry. Thanks for the promise of teens, Fritz."

A partially burned raccoon coat lay on the ground at the side of the cabin—a reminder of the *Hindenburg* disaster and an omen of a nightmare that lay ahead.

Amelia

"I'm so glad to be with you and get to know you! Theo said you fly airplanes and even do stunts!"

Amelia Earhart never turned her eyes from the rough road as she gripped the steering wheel of her military issued Jeep, but a smile graced her face. "Well, Gracie, after my letter from Jahile came from Germany, I could scarcely wait to meet you two! It sounds like you are brave adventurers." A sharp bark nipped the air from the backseat. "Oh, and of course, Murphy, you must be a brave warrior dog too! Forgive me for leaving you out!" Her playful words made all laugh as Murphy leaned his head over the side of the car and let the wind blow his ears.

"Actually, Ms. Earhart…"

"Amelia," the round-faced woman interrupted and threw a glance over her shoulder at Theo in the open backseat. "Just call me Amelia."

Theo let out a short chuckle. He wondered how he could feel so comfortable with someone he just met—especially when the "someone" was well-known, talented, fearless, and a woman on top of all that. "Okay, um, Amelia, I don't know how you do airplane stunts. After walking across the suspension bridge from the *Hindenburg* to the engine car, I never again want to be so high up without something underneath in case I fall!"

Amelia and Gracie both laughed. Amelia had a warm, tinkling laugh as light as the wind and very contagious.

"Besides, all women in this Jeep need to be nice to me today."

Gracie turned and squealed, "What! We're always nice to you. Right, Amelia?" Giggles from the front of the Jeep rolled with the wind. "So, Theo, Why? Give us one reason we have to be nice to you today." She winked as her curls bounced around her pretty face.

"Because today's my eighteenth birthday. I'm a man today."

Laughter mixed with Gracie's whoops satisfied Theo. He had never heard a better chorus of the birthday song than belted out by their new friend Amelia.

"Aw, thanks, Miss Amelia. You two sure know how to make a guy feel special."

Amelia lifted both hands from the steering wheel for a brief moment. "I better keep my hands on the wheel, or you'll wonder if my flying is as bad as my driving!"

"Naw, we're not worried, are we, Gracie?" Theo reached up and gave a soft squeeze to Gracie's shoulder.

"Anyway, Amelia, I read about you in my history...um in my list of news accounts. Uh-hum." Theo cleared his throat after catching his near mistake. "Um, your flights are interesting. By the way, did you ever meet Bessie Coleman?"

"Bessie!" Amelia's eyes flashed another quick glance over her shoulder to get a brief look at Theo. "Ah, what a wonderful woman! Meet her? I loved her dearly. She was such a talented stunt pilot! Oh, I do miss her!"

Gracie knit her eyebrows and tilted her head to look at Amelia, so Theo knew his tiny friend was deep in thought. "There aren't a lot of women in flying. I hope they're good to you and Bessie."

"Oh, most men in the flight industry are more than kind—once they understand that a freckle-face kid like me isn't going to be satisfied playing with dolls. I'm not sure how Bessie got her start. She had three strikes against her as a black woman stunt pilot. As for me, I had already kinda broken the stereotype of women's careers, anyway. My first love was medicine. I was a nurse aide in Toronto during the war. That was where I realized that whether I became a doctor or flew airplanes, my heart and my mind were made up—nursing was not going to be my career forever."

"So, were you and Bessie the first women in flight?" Theo knew that women didn't often step into men's careers, especially in the world of the 1930s.

"No, actually, my flight instructor was a woman."

"Really?" Gracie almost bounced on the seat of the bumpy Jeep.

"Really. So, Gracie, from what Jahile has said about you, I have a feeling that you follow your heart and not just what someone—even some leader—has said you should do."

"Hello. Murphy and I are feeling a little awkward here." Theo gave a little singsong tease from the backseat of the Jeep.

"Well, my advice is the same for you, Theo. I think you've experienced enough to know your motivation comes from within your soul. Mavericks make a difference"—Amelia twisted the side of her mouth in a pause of thought—"maybe good, maybe bad—not for the sake of changing the rules but by ignoring society's boundaries, the heart can take a flying leap."

"I guess for you that flying leap was literal." Theo was quick to play on words, and all three in the Jeep laughed into the swift-moving air of the road.

"Will you fly again soon? Maybe we can watch you take off. Maybe we can see you land. Theo said you have a yellow plane. Will you fly your yellow plane?" Gracie's questions rolled out with every bump in the road before Amelia had a chance to answer. Again, the tinkling laugh bubbled from the depths of Amelia's soul.

Though he sat in the middle of the bench seat, Theo could reach his long arms from one side of the Jeep to the other to brace his bounces. Eventually, the military issue found smooth pavement of highway that took off down the eastern seaboard toward the Capitol.

"So many questions! I'm afraid you think I'm some kind of superwoman. But to answer your question, yes. I have my first flight around the world scheduled for next month. It should be thrilling, but I have some business to wrap up before I'm gone for such a long flight."

Miles and time passed quickly while the four passengers enjoyed the fresh air and conversation until Amelia maneuvered through the streets of Washington, DC where Theo and Gracie's new friend interrupted their sightseeing. "Now, let's put this conversation back into a hangar so you can meet a dear friend of mine. If you don't mind, I'd like to carry Murphy. He's quite a personable dog, and I'm too busy to have one of my own right now."

The Jeep came to a stop at a large white house at 1600 Pennsylvania Avenue.

A Nation Past

"California? That's just the western coastline of the States of America."

Mrs. Roosevelt turned her head slowly, letting her upper torso lean toward Theo who sat expressionless. "What did you say, young man?" Her soft voice was not accusatory, but something in the tone caught Gracie's curiosity, so she, too, looked at Theo.

"In talking to Ms. Earhart about her flights just now, you said from Maine to California, ma'am. Well, Maine is a state, but California is just a narrow strip of land that shows where the states end and the Pacific Ocean begins." Theo spoke matter-of-factly as he moved his eyes from the lady of the White House in an arc around the small circle of people in the room. "You know, you seemed to, I mean, I thought you were calling California a state. That's all." Theo shifted in the overstuffed chair and patted his leg to call Murphy to sit beside him as he became a little uneasy with the sudden silence in the room.

"No offense taken, young man, but someone of your age should know the United States a little better. If we don't understand the geography of our own country, we can hardly be expected to understand the foreign places to which we wish to travel or have political ties." Mrs. Roosevelt reached over and patted Theo's arm to express her kindness. "I'm sure you know the United States. You've been through a lot from what Amelia tells me, and I don't want you to be flustered."

Theo straightened a little in his chair. "I…I'm, uh, sorry, ma'am, but I'm not sure we're talking about the same thing. Mr. Medi, uh, my history teacher, uh, he spoke about the United States, but that was in our past history unit." He looked around the room and held both arms suspended in air as if to suggest he didn't understand. His vision moved from Gracie back to Mrs. Roosevelt while he blinked hard and dropped his hands to his lap. "Oh my gosh! I'm so sorry. I forgot I *am* in the past right now!" He looked straight into the eyes of the First Lady. "Mrs. Roosevelt, you must think I don't know my history, but I do! I was just a little confused for a minute."

Eleanor Roosevelt lifted her chin as if to tilt Theo's words further back into her mind. "Theo"—she paused and turned her head—"Gracie, I am a woman of intelligence. My husband's political position requires me to think before I speak and to ensure that I consider what I hear with rationality and common sense." She adjusted her gloved hands in her lap and returned her gaze to the young man beside her. "Theo, my dear Amelia has told me of your claims to have lived in the future."

Theo placed Murphy on his lap and gave a quick head rub that made the dog's ears flap back and forth. "It's true, ma'am. I can show you so many—"

A gloved hand with an index finger pointing toward the ceiling came into Theo's line of sight. "Fine, Theo, fine." Eleanor Roosevelt dropped her hand back to her lap. "Let's just say for the sake of curiosity, dear young man, that you tell me a little about the future of our country—no fairy tales or apocryphal stories—just what you know to be true."

Theo knew that to win back credibility, he would need to pull from the lessons of his history class and lead into the America where he lived with his father, robotic dog, and integrated robotic intelligence system, IRIS, who had been created to serve as their housemaid and servant. "Well, ma'am, Ms. Earhart..." Theo looked at the women with curiosity on their faces before he turned to look at Gracie whose expression showed she had no knowledge of America but whose smiling eyes showed support for whatever he had to say. Theo swallowed the lump in his throat and patted the dog lying draped across his lap. "Well, the states you speak of, I know there had been as many as fifty of them at one time."

"At one time?" Mrs. Roosevelt caught her interruption. "I'm sorry, Theo, continue."

"Um, yes, ma'am. The States of America is not the same country from the twentieth century that the history books talk about." Theo noticed a slight upturn of Mrs. Roosevelt's face and raise of her eyebrows, indicating a mix of disbelief and of wanting to hear more.

"Actually, it wasn't until the twenty-first century, the century I live in…uh, I mean the century I came from, that some states started changing."

"Changing?" Amelia Earhart spoke with a furrowed brow.

Theo combined a deep sigh with a nod of his head. "After quite a political debacle in the twenty-first century, a state called Texas chose to secede from the group—sorry, I mean, the union—of fifty states. Now, uh, I mean, in the twenty-first century, Texas is its own independent republic. One state called Oklahoma decided to leave with them, but only half of the land territory went with the Republic of Texas." Theo wanted to express the truth he knew in a positive light. "According to Mr. Medi—uh, he's my history teacher in school—it sounds like the Republic of Texas is strong and well-liked by other nations." He could tell his voice had risen in pitch, so he took a deep breath to keep from sounding like an excited schoolboy.

"Another state in the Pacific Ocean, Hawaii, wanted to go back to its roots and rejoin other Polynesian countries, but after being detached from the economy of the states for a year, the ruling officials of the Hawaiian Islands begged to be rejoined. The decision was put to a vote both by the colony of America and by China before they held a day of amnesty and renamed Hawaii as part of the States of America."

"Colony? What colony? And why would China have a voice?" This time Amelia spoke up and shifted uncomfortably in her chair. "You seem to be weaving tales, young man."

"Oh, no! Please, I tell the truth!" Theo shook his head as he looked back and forth between the two women.

"Continue." Mrs. Roosevelt spoke barely above a whisper. "Be careful with your word choice. What other states left the Union?"

"Union? Oh, you mean the states? Well, just past the democratic government's demise, other states left the union. New Mexico drew a border halfway up the state, taking strips of Colorado and

Kansas, too, making a fuzzy border between Mexico and the States, while other states just went away."

"Went away?"

"Yes, Mrs. Roosevelt. Erosion of land narrowed the state of California until all that's left is the border of the Pacific west coast. Most of California, just like the states chewed away by the Gulf waters, lies under ocean waters."

"And your use of terms—colony, China—please explain, young man." Mrs. Roosevelt gave no impression she believed his explanation, but she prompted him forward.

"Well, if I remember what Mr. Medi told us, your America is called the *United* States of America." Theo waited while Mrs. Roosevelt nodded in agreement.

Sensing that what he had to say would not be popular with the wife of a president, Theo continued with a voice of compassion. "The Debacle of Demise, as the unrest of the twenty-first century is called, caused so much distrust between the people and the government that even people within each state started turning on each other. The concept of unity dissolved. States were fighting to keep peace within their own borders and to stay afloat on financial debt to the nation. The White House sold out to other countries. China came to the rescue, and the term *united* was dropped.

"At first people rebelled against being controlled by another country. China wasn't the only country trying to take the nation, but it proved the most financial ownership, and the States of America had no defense. So, China is now the mother country, making America a colony to her."

When Theo looked back at Mrs. Roosevelt, she was no longer looking at him but rather had turned her gaze to a corner of the ceiling. Even though her eyes looked away, Gracie was certain a glittery wetness rimmed the corners of Mrs. Roosevelt's eyes.

"Are you happy?" Mrs. Roosevelt spoke softly without looking back at her visitors.

"Yeah, I guess so. I mean, I hear my dad complain about government restrictions every once in a while, and Mr. Medi talks about how people were allowed to travel around the country before the debacle, but we all have jobs and stuff. People without jobs are sent to locations in Utah and Arizona, so I guess the government takes care of them. The news is audited and controlled by China, but the news doesn't report that we're *not* happy." Theo wrinkled his forehead, not sure if he was even convincing himself.

Silence hung in the blue carpeted room until Mrs. Roosevelt stood and smiled at Theo and Gracie as if they had just walked in the door. She glanced at Amelia and lifted a small brass bell from a marble table beside her chair. "Amelia, I think we should feed these dear people." She turned back to smile at the two teens as she gently shook the bell, rousing Murphy from his sleep with a jerk that flung him off Theo's lap with a thud onto the floor. Everyone laughed as Murphy pearl hopped in a circle to fend off any attackers.

As if the bell's clapper were tied to the doorknob, the tall door opened to a man standing in a pressed suit. "Josiah, please escort our dear friends to the nook off the kitchen so they can have a bite to eat. I'm sure they're famished! Oh, and, Josiah, give them a personal tour while they're here. Especially see that they have some private time to clean up and rest in the guest rooms. Have them back to the dining room for a snack before bed and some time to themselves. They've had a long day arriving in *the United States*." Stressing her last words, Eleanor winked at Theo and smiled. She let an extended arm swing toward her friend. "Amelia and I will be out enjoying the spring evening in the garden. Theo, Gracie, enjoy your time."

With a movement of graceful ease, Mrs. Roosevelt turned and moved across the blue carpet toward the door. "There's always time for talk."

The First Lady paused in the doorway and swiveled half around. "Theo, does Murphy need time outside to do 'his business'?"

"Oh no, thank you, ma'am. He doesn't need to, I, um, mean, he's okay for now."

Murphy sat looking at the people in the room by cocking his head from side to side, wondering what they were saying.

Warnings

A dark cloud seeped into the closed room. Murphy scooted with his nose along the bottom of the door. His wagging tail froze as a low growl vibrated the furry robot. Theo looked across the room, lit only by daylight where the heavy curtains split to an open window.

"Murph." Theo's gravelly whisper brought no response. "Murphy. Hey, Murph. What's up, boy?" He knew the robot dog was programmed to growl only to alert of danger. "We're okay here, Murph. This is America." He shook his head, not understanding why his tongue felt so thick and his words sounded slurred. Suddenly, his hand grasped his own neck that jerked from a stab of pain in the night air.

A putrid smell filled the air as the black smoke crawled and formed an opaque pillar. Murphy's on-point growl faded behind the dark smoke. Then, as if taking on a life-form of its own, the pillar twisted and arched over the small dog.

Theo lurched toward Murphy. "Nooo! Murphy! Run!" In slow motion, he swung his arms through the air trying to grasp the dark cloud. The smoke snaked around Murphy's neck and tightened, lifting the dog off the ground by his neck, moving him toward the open window.

Murphy's growl changed to whimpers as his robotic legs kicked against nothing in midair.

"STOP!" Theo's voice sounded muffled in his ears, though he knew he was yelling with every breath of air in his lungs. He tried to grab Murphy's legs and missed as the black smoke and Murphy disappeared through the open window.

A COLD NOSE NUDGED THEO's cheek causing him to spring from the bed where he had fallen asleep.

"Augh!" Theo lunged to the window and slammed his palms against the closed glass. He twisted toward the bed and saw his companion sitting, wagging his tail where Theo had just been napping. "Murphy! You're here! You're not gone!" He moved to the middle of the room and spun in place. "There's no smoke. Oh, Murphy, you're here!" The young man fell toward the bed and wrapped both arms around the dog sitting with his head cocked in confusion.

The petting stopped when Murphy nudged his master's neck. Theo rolled back across the bed looking up at the ceiling. "It all seemed so real." He looked at Murphy and again ran his hand down the dog's back. "Too real, Murphy. I guess it was just a nightmare. It can't be another premonition. It just can't be." He rested one arm across his forehead to press back the headache behind his eyes. With his other hand, he rubbed his neck. "It just can't be. Something felt like it punched through my neck. Then I saw smoke—something—I don't know, but somehow the smoke had you around the neck, Murphy, holding your collar as it took you…"

Murphy had just snuggled down beside his master when Theo jerked upright. "Your collar! Murphy, your collar has information from your spy mission on the *Hindenburg*!" Murphy raised his eyebrows to give a look of interest to his master though his senses had no programming to understand how to return feelings of excitement.

Theo spoke to Murphy as if trying to talk to a child. "Remember when I let the two little boys on the *Hindenburg* play with you? Well, it wasn't exactly you, as a dog, but it was you. Remember Walter and Werner? Those two boys were sad when their toy tank was taken by the *Hindenburg* crewman. I had you roll into your silver ball so they could have a new toy." Theo took a quick breath while Murphy cocked his head. "Except the plan wasn't for you to be a toy. I mean, yeah, you were a toy for the boys, but you were to be a spy to hear talk where the boys were playing." He gave a quick rub to Murphy's head before he began chattering again.

"I have no idea where you were or what you heard. The *Hindenburg* crashed and all stuff broke loose before Amelia brought us here. So you see, little buddy, I haven't listened to the recording chip in your collar! Maybe my bad dream was just a wake-up call to see what you know!"

Murphy didn't "see" why Theo smiled, but it seemed like a good time to snort and bury his nose in the covers.

"Don't mind me, Murph. I just need some time with your collar." Theo removed the collar from Murphy's neck as the beagle rolled to his side. "Okay. Snore away. I don't mind hearing your system recharge."

Somewhere in the wilderness or streets of Germany Theo had lost his handy all-purpose tool. He tugged on the lanyard around his neck and dangled the driftboard charm. The bent charm had been his makeshift screwdriver since Gracie had once used it to pick a lock.

"Okay, little charm. Just pop open this collar and…" The slender teen had grown into a man's size since his time jump. "Zikes. I can't even get my finger inside this collar box anymore." He put the charm in a divot on the chip and gave a half-turn. "Yeah, there we go." He covered the chip with his wrist computer. In colorful waves the quantum phonons danced across the computer watch and voices came to life. A tap on the last recorded entry, May 6, 1937, brought words from the *Hindenburg* to life.

> *"Such a beautiful raccoon coat with a devil inside."*
> *"My dear, are you upset that our dealing with a German spy might damage your idea of style?"*
> *"Well, my sweet, you have to admit he must have a good position in the Reich to afford a coat like that. I care nothing for the man, but I do wish you had a beautiful coat like that."*

Theo moved the computer chip to pause the voices. "Raccoon coat?" Theo spoke into the silent air. "I remember seeing a man wearing a raccoon coat on the *Hindenburg*. Besides those sitting beside the viewing windows, most people didn't wear coats in the lounge or dining areas. Hmm. I wish I could remember his face, but I just remember seeing the back of his coat. Seems like he was always on the move when I came into a room." Theo shook his head.

"Uh-huh. Makes sense why he wouldn't want to stay in one place for long. A spy. Ugh." He shivered. "Maybe one of Viktor Brack's minions." Theo reached over and slid his hand down the back of the sleeping dog. "Okay, not a minion since he had an expensive coat, but definitely someone on Brack's side."

"But I did hear what the man and woman called him—a spy! Okay, shh!" Theo shushed the sleeping dog and moved the watch over the computer chip again.

> *"I'm not sure he's one we need to avoid."*
>
> *"What? Don't we consider most Germans on this airship as probable spies?"*
>
> *"Of course, my dear."* A pause in the man's speaking caused Theo to lift his wrist computer closer to his earbud as if keeping the recording a secret.
>
> *"Surely the Reich is smart enough to know it's not just Americans they have to fear. We'd be foolish to assume the Germans don't know Red Peace is aboard. Our society is—"*
>
> *"Hush, now!"* the man's voice interrupted softly before raising a bit. *"Boys! Why don't you play in the corner again? What happened to that silver ball you were rolling? Now go play. We have a right to visit without your interruptions."* The man cleared his throat.
>
> *"Oh, really, now. I think you've frightened the boys. Sometimes I think you suspect everyone as an*

enemy ready to eavesdrop on all of your plans with Red Peace."

"Never can be too cautious, my dear." Again the man's voice changed pitch. *"Just be happy I don't suspicion you."*

Theo heard light chuckles follow the man's remark, yet it didn't seem like happy laughter.

The sound of the man inhaling prompted his speaking.

"Oh, darling. You are a perfect spy for Red Peace, the best I've ever known because of your innocent beauty. I do agree that the man in the coat is a spy. I just don't think he's working with Red Peace on his radar."

"Who else would he care about? He doesn't dine anywhere close to the American tables."

"Not sure, my dear, but I have caught sight of him twice talking to a German cabin boy, tall kid, kind of awkward, and not really helpful when I've asked him for service."

"So you think the cabin boy is a plant too? Interesting. But if they're not interested in us, who are they trailing?"

"More than once I've seen both the boy and the man watching and ducking behind walls and corners when a pretty little dark-skinned girl enters the room, at least I think she's a girl. Curls hang from below a cap she wears. She wears heavy boots and dungarees, but I've seen her looking the Doehner girl up and down."

"Doehner? What would their daughter have to do with anything?"

"Well, forgive me dear for what I'm about to say, but the look in the eyes of the dark-skinned girl *have a, hmm, shall I say piercing look toward the Doehner girl."*

"Piercing? You mean like a jealousy?" Light laughter followed, this time in a happy tone.

Again, Theo paused the recording. "You go, Gracie. I knew you were jealous! Ha! That's my little angel. Oh, I hope you weren't a devilish angel making sweet Irene miserable." Theo gave his heart time to enjoy the warmth of Gracie's attention before he moved the chip under the watch and listened.

The woman's voice continued.
"I've brushed past that coat closely enough that I could feel the soft fur. I do know it only carries the scent of a man's cologne."
"You confuse me with your woman talk, my dear. Does the smell of his coat really matter?"
"No." Again there was a pause and a sound of shuffling made as the fabric of the woman's dress moved against the cushioned chair.
"No, but when we were setting the, uh-hum, the trunk on the walkway, do you remember how we glanced at each other before we quickly left? I was nearly overcome by that horrible smell."

Theo swallowed and shook his head as if responding to the voice on the recording chip. "Yep. Jaegers. So these people were from the Russian *Red Peace* society, and jaegers found them putting a trunk on…" Theo gasped. "We did see it! Murphy, we did see a trunk on the walkway! Help me remember to tell Gracie. We did see it, but when we told Joseph and Erich and took them to the catwalk, the trunk was gone!"

The voices interrupted Theo's thoughts.

"Come, dear, we mustn't be late for dinner. We'll rearrange the location of the trunk as we planned,

then refresh ourselves so we are seen coming from our room as all move toward the dining room."

"Oh, Murphy! The trunk! *These people!*" Theo pointed to the face of his wrist computer. *"Red Peace?* Was the fire on the *Hindenburg* an accident? What happened, Murphy? Oh, I gotta share this with President Roosevelt! I remember Mr. Medi's lecture in history class where he suggested the crash of the *Hindenburg* was suspicious, but I don't remem…"

Noise from the wrist computer was a cacophony of boys' voices and sounds of people passing through rooms and halls before it cleared into the recorded conversation of men, voices different than before.

"Who was on duty to watch the cargo hold?" The voice of the SS officer on the recording was terse but not loud.

"I haven't seen him. It was a jaeger. I started missing his blasted smell last night. Since then, I've discreetly searched through the cargo hold where we held our meeting to discuss this escapade. No luck there. I've even searched a couple cargo holds farther back."

A sound of disgust followed.

"I've never known one to go missing or disobey a direct order like this before."

Theo gasped, "A missing jaeger? The one Gracie stabbed in the eye with the screwdriver? The one we…" He struggled to admit the truth. His voice was no more than a breath of sound. "The one we *killed?*" He adjusted the earbud in his ear.

"I'll go after dinner and check the cargo holds again. I'll set the other two on that rigger—Erich, I think is his name—and get some answers as soon as I can."

"Excellent. If he's working for who we think he is, then he should be able to answer a few important questions. Keep up appearances during dinner then slip out as soon as you think no one will be suspicious."

"Sir. Heil Hitler."

Theo visualized a salute to the officer.

The recording scratched with boots shuffling and a dull thud.

From where he rested on the bed, Murphy jumped into perfect on-point form with a lip lifted in a soft growl, his eyes fixed on Theo's computer watch.

Theo ran a hand down the raised hackles on Murphy's neck. "Whoa, boy. It's okay. Whatever made that thud sure got under your skin! You did a great job of recording, ol' boy." Theo patted Murphy as the dog's growl faded into the silence of the wrist screen. "Sorry, boy. You must have had something unpleasant happen, but you're okay now. You're okay now, buddy."

Theo replaced the collar before he nestled his face into Murphy's fur. "You're okay, now."

A Task at Hand

Gracie rolled from the soft bed and crossed the floor to look at the morning outside the bay window. Instinctively, she put her palm against the windowpane. The roses in the garden below were so vibrant that if the window had no glass, she was sure she would touch and smell every petal. She leaned her forehead against the glass, letting her face turn until her cheek lay against the cool windowpane. Her eye caught sight of her rough, unmanicured fingernails. On the streets of Munich, her rough hands had never bothered her, but she had noticed other hands and wondered if Theo had noticed too.

I'll never have soft hands like the Lady of Eltz Castle or Amelia or even Irene. A knot had swollen in Gracie's throat from the thought of the sweet girl named Irene. The girl with such innocent charm, who had suffered by Gracie's threatening words of jealousy and who had died so horribly in the crash of the *Hindenburg*. She let her thoughts unfairly chastise her. *I'll never be a beautiful and soft woman. Why would Theo ever want to be with me?* A bird hopped to the windowsill and cocked its head allowing a tiny bead of an eye to look at her face. Gracie tapped the pane with a finger.

"Hello, sweet bird. You have a beautiful home." The bird flew away, letting a downy white feather fall onto the ledge outside the window. Gracie pushed back from where she lay against the window. As if the wings of the bird fanned fresh air to her soul, Gracie looked around the room until her eyes fell on a washstand with a porcelain bowl and pitcher.

"Well, *Fräulein*, you're in a new country with new adventure ahead. This is a good time to start being a new girl." Gracie stepped lightly across the room to freshen up with water and new clothes that had been brought in by a maid. She spoke to the reflection in the washstand mirror. "We'll see what Theo thinks of you today!" By the time of her first breakfast in America, she was certain she could love this country far from home and love everybody in it.

Breakfast in the White House came with pampering—a smorgasbord of food, laughs, and stories of America and Germany. To the teens, it was as close to being with saints in heaven as could be imagined with nothing sad and nothing to bring harm. Yet the air in the room filled with a somber silence when the chairs were pushed back and Mrs. Roosevelt invited the teens and Amelia into her private parlor.

"Theo, Gracie, I cannot tell you how much it warms my heart to meet you and have your laughter and friendship within these walls. You have met all of my hopes for American youth"—the First Lady paused and folded her hands—"even though neither of you are American from today's world." Smiles passed between faces, but minds remained alert and uncertain of where Mrs. Roosevelt was heading.

Amelia recognized the looks of cautious anticipation and stepped in to help her friend initiate the conversation behind private doors. "Theo and Gracie"—she nodded at each in turn—"my dear friend Jahile spoke true of you." She paused as she unfolded a paper pulled from her pocket and began to read.

>*Dearest Amelia,*
>
>*Today I think of you and the work you do in America in the stand for what is right. Like Esther in the Bible, I believe you make use of your position and contacts "for such a time as this." I admire you and thank you and support you.*
>
>*Now, my dear friend, I wish to introduce you to two of the finest youths of today. Like us, they have a heart and a passion for what is right. They didn't choose this path. Circumstance has brought them together. They are strong, and they are willing to stand for right. For fear of interception of this let-*

ter, I will only mention their first names, Theo and Gracie, and ask you to welcome them and see that they are delivered to their journey's end in America. I will not be surprised, however, if they choose to help you in any of your "needs" while they are in your company.

Treat them kindly as if you are treating a piece of my heart, for surely that is where they reside with me.

Dark Victory,
Jahile

PS Welcome also their dog as he is a mighty force to bind hearts though he is small in stature.

No one spoke as Amelia folded the letter and tucked it back into the pocket of her flight uniform. Theo saw Gracie's long curls fall forward as her head bowed and her hands raised to cover her eyes. For once, he was not uncomfortable or hesitant in sliding to Gracie's side to wrap an arm around her shoulders to touch his forehead against hers. Patiently and attentively, both American women watched the two teens react to the words of their dear guardian.

Murphy had quietly been sitting beside the feet of the First Lady. Though a robot without feeling or emotion, he had been created to recognize anyone who would bring no harm to his master. A heavy silence blanketed the room, interrupted only by an intermittent sniffle from the teens. Murphy's usual trotting click could not be heard as he padded across the wool carpet to nestle between the feet of his master.

Through stinging eyes Theo looked at Amelia. "When was that letter written?"

"Written?" Amelia again pulled the letter from her pocket and searched for an answer. "Here it is, at the top, April 1937." She lowered the letter and tipped her head. "Does the date have significance?"

Neither Theo nor Gracie had mentioned Herr Möeller more than briefly in their initial conversation with Mrs. Roosevelt. They had not considered any closeness Amelia held with their guardian or that she would know about his capture by the Reich.

"Oh, Amelia!" Gracie's heart burst into sobs. "He's been taken! They've taken him!" She crumbled into Theo's arms.

Amelia unknowingly fisted her hand that held the letter from Jahile. "What? No! Oh, children! Oh, my Jahile!" She stood and turned her back to all sitting in a tight circle in the private room. Soft tiny curls bobbed with her shaking shoulders as she shared the teens' sorrow. She spoke softly without turning to face anyone. "We know, we know from the time we take a stand that we are opposed and not without consequence. We know, and so we deliberately stand. Still, it hurts when one of our own is taken." Her voice strengthened, and her head tipped back as her voice rose to the ceiling. "They may have taken him, but they will never break his spirit! He'll never forsake the good! They may have him, but they will never have his soul or the memory any of us have of him! Oh, that we may all stand as Jahile has stood! Oh, oh, I must get word to my dear George!"

Again a silence hung in the room until Eleanor stood and spoke with a firm voice, "I see you are all touched by the life of one good man. Perhaps you will understand, then, why I must meet with you today." She walked to the woman who stood with her back to them. "Amelia, give me a little time to meet with the children on the issue you and I have discussed. You must find your husband and tell him what you have learned. George will want to know, and he will comfort you in this unwanted news."

Theo looked up at the First Lady. She looked every bit of her fifty-plus years, and she really didn't seem to have beauty pageant qualities, but there was something that drew people to her. He noticed Mrs. Roosevelt's eyes would watch whoever was speaking, and she often had a long pause before talking, a pause that people were willing to endure. Theo watched the First Lady and bit his lip in thought.

I like her. She doesn't remind me of my mother. No, she's too old. But I like her. She seems so gentle, but I bet she stands her ground. I don't have a grandmother, so why am I drawn to her? She's... Theo's eyes watched her hands give a gentle squeeze to Amelia's shoulders. He watched her walk to the drapes and pull them closed. He watched her move a plate of cookies from a sideboard to the small table in the center of the circle where they sat—cookies offered in gesture of hospitality, cookies that looked delicious, but cookies that sat untouched until they were dumped by a butler later in the day.

She's like…you know, I think she's like my integrated robot information system back home. Yes. Theo inconspicuously nodded as he released Gracie and returned to his chair. *If I ever put a face on my robot maid, IRIS, she would have to look just like Eleanor Roosevelt. They're both intelligent, determined to do what is right, and know just what to say. Humph. When I get home, I'll ask IRIS what she knows about Mrs. Roosevelt, then I'll tease her and call her Eleanor instead of IRIS. I bet she'll take it as a compliment.*

"Dear Amelia"—Eleanor twisted around to smile at the young woman—"go ahead. Find your sweet George. There's so much you two have to do to prepare for your flight around the world next month. You have served me and your country well. It's time for you to follow the flight path of your heart."

Lost in thought, Theo didn't notice when Amelia left and the First Lady returned to her chair. Eleanor sat down, quietly smoothing the folds in the skirt of her dress. A heavy pat of the gracious lady's hand against her lap snapped Theo from his daydream.

"All right," Mrs. Roosevelt spoke firmly without raising the sound of her voice beyond the three of them in the circle of chairs. "I've been given some information—though I have my own suspicions—and I have a plan. However"—she paused and looked directly at Theo and Gracie before speaking again—"I would like to hear a few details from you. I hope you don't mind my questions. I think we can work together, but I can't go off half-cocked and miss my target." Mrs. Roosevelt winked at Theo who smiled with the metaphor though Gracie didn't understand why the First Lady had decided to talk about guns.

Theo looked at Gracie and bent over his arm tucked against his stomach as if bowing from where he sat. "Ladies first." He swung his other arm in Gracie's direction.

Gracie looked at the grinning friend beside her and smiled back. *One look at him, and I either want to run away or melt. Ugh! How can he be so silly and sweet one minute and make me want to pinch him the next! Maybe at first I wasn't sure about him, but now I know how I feel. There's something about him that makes me...*

"Gracie? Is that all right with you?"

Mrs. Roosevelt's question popped the bubble forming around Gracie's heart and reminded her that she was being watched by all in the room.

"Oh, sorry. I guess I was..." Everyone's soft laughter set her at ease.

Gracie began with the night when her papa, Grey Cooper, took her to Jahile Möeller's home. She didn't leave out important details, including her rebellious behavior against her papa's German friend. "Honestly, I don't know why Herr Möeller always came to my rescue and put up with my bitter words. But he did. He did. He cared for me as if I were his own daughter"—she pointed to the chair beside hers—"and Theo too! Well, not like a daughter, but like a son." Her correction made everyone laugh, everyone except Murphy who gave a puppy sigh and spun three circles until he collapsed into sleep.

"Yeah! Then I came into the picture the same way Gracie did. I got beaten up and needed help." Theo lunged into his explanation of his first days in Germany, beginning with the TimeWorm jump. His words revived memories of the concentration camp filled with Jewish children, and his heart honored those who first saved his life in Germany—Yari, Emilie Schindler, and Maximilian Kolbe. He still reckoned with the days that took him from an egocentric boy to a young man who woke to the real heroes of life.

Sharing their venture with words that tumbled out across the woolen carpet, Theo and Gracie told of their rescues and rescuers from Jahile Möeller to Joseph Späh. At times their voices built in intensity, and at times they blurted out the same words as they interrupted to fill in detail or finish each other's sentences. The teens ended with their story resting at the base of the burning dirigible and their hands gripping the other's, unaware they had moved toward each other.

Through it all, Mrs. Roosevelt's kind, yet expressionless face held eyes that recorded into her memory all they said.

"What a journey!" Eleanor's words came with honesty, buoyed out on a sigh. "I admire you two. Your fortitude has had great mentors. I suppose you realize, you've learned from the best. There are, Theo, a few more questions I need answered if you don't mind."

"Uh, sure!" Theo treasured their honesty with America's First Lady.

"Your story before Germany, when you lived in the future. Honestly, to speak of moving from the future to today seems a little preposterous, but a man named H. G. Wells wrote—"

Theo held up a finger to signal his interruption. "Yeah, okay. I mean, yes, ma'am. I'm familiar with H. G. Wells. He wrote fiction. In all respect, ma'am, my life actually happened. It may not seem believable, but here's the truth."

Theo sat back in the parlor chair and told about IRIS, his dad's life as a scientist, the TimeWorm machine, and even some of Murphy's robotics. He was surprised how Mrs. Roosevelt's expression never changed, even when he was sure some of the technology and science would seem unbelievable. She looked as if she were memorizing every point Theo made. Gracie's bright eyes suggested she was hearing every detail for the first time, though in Herr Möeller's home, she had listened to Theo's stories.

Gracie turned her head to the fidgeting First Lady, and Theo hesitated a few times when Eleanor showed discomfort in hearing the name of Viktor Brack.

Talking for long periods of time had never been a habit for Theo, but it was Mrs. Roosevelt who breathed a long audible sigh when the young man from America finished his story.

"Very well." Mrs. Roosevelt interrupted a long silence that followed Theo's explanation of the time jump. "You have traveled a difficult road during your sojourn in this decade and in Germany. I would ask that you"—the First Lady turned her head to Gracie—"you and Gracie, consider how you can help me before you continue on your personal journey."

She stood and walked to a small desk in the parlor and shuffled through a drawer before she returned to stand in front of her visitors. "It's no secret here in America that the führer and anyone tied to the Third Reich holds only hatred for my husband as President of the United States. Franklin is an intelligent man who pursues the good of this country and relationships with other countries, those who are good and also those who threaten the world. There are German immigrants here in America"—Eleanor caught her mistake—"oh, not all of them. You can never put one label on an entire country. Yet, there are immigrants who would take away the free will of a man. But many, too many immigrants from Germany want to live on American soil but stand under the ruling rod of Adolf Hitler."

Theo had never realized how harshly the name the führer could be spoken. He rolled the name of Viktor Brack around in his mind and wondered how the character of a man could shape his name into a harsh sound.

Mrs. Roosevelt tipped her chin upward to look out from under her eyebrows. "Many immigrants are raising their children with insurrection in their hearts. They want their children to eat from the American table of plenty without professing a love for the freedom that gives them such opportunity. As a result, there are camps for German youth springing up in overwhelming numbers. They spread across our country, but most are located here in the East. They claim to promote bonding through a summer camp. However, our government suspicions that these camps are building a generation of anarchists."

The First Lady paused long enough to relax the tension in her face and smile at the two teens. "This is where you may be able to help. We, Franklin and I, will not force you to help us, but we know you and your families have suffered from the hand of the Third Reich. We have heard that freedom is a passion that pulses through your veins. We ask you to help us infiltrate a German camp so we can know with absolute assurance whether or not we should be fearful of a power attacking from within." She cocked her head and looked at Theo. "Perhaps that is what happened in your world that stole

America's freedom and placed her in servitude under China." She pursed her lips and looked away, quietly shaking her head.

The proposal seemed coated with a million questions. When Jahile Möeller shared his plan to get both teens to America, Theo had intended a step onto 1937 American soil then catapult into the future with the spinning orbs of the TimeWorm. His heart was committed to the people of his past, but now his mind wanted to return home, a home not only in place but also in time. His thoughts were interrupted.

"Theo, for you, I'm sure there is quite a bit to consider. Think of what I have asked. I leave you to yourselves today, and we'll meet for an answer after dinner this evening. For now, you must explore Washington while I attend a meeting of a women's organization.

With a nod and smile, Eleanor Roosevelt opened the door of her private parlor and gestured that the meeting had ended.

Preparation

"Hurrah for those who stand against the annihilation of non-Aryans by Hitler's Third Reich." Theo spoke into the bathroom mirror, wondering when his face had broadened. A year ago, he had never gone a week without shaving, but his face boasted a substantial amount of hair growth that had gone months without grooming before he was smuggled onto the *Hindenburg*. "Again, the fuzzy face of a man appears; yet to be stroked back into childhood! Heil, razor!" In mock jest, Theo held out the razor until it almost touched the mirror.

The clean-shaven young man met Gracie in the hall before escorting her to the second floor dining room. Theo suppressed a huge smile into a welcoming grin in response to a nod and raised eyebrow offered by the girl he wanted to please. She didn't leave his efforts without reward.

"Mmm. That looks nice." Gracie reached up and let the back of her hand drag down the side of Theo's face. "I can't decide if I like you best with or without a beard."

"Doesn't matter as long as you like—"

"This way, friends!"

More disappointed than startled, Theo was interrupted by a house butler.

"The president has a meeting, but Mrs. Roosevelt has convinced him a muffin or two shared with you at breakfast will be a treat for him. He'll share a quick bite before he has to dismiss himself." The butler gestured toward the open doorway at the end of the hall as if Theo and Gracie were royalty visiting the White House.

RENDERED

"Good morning!" Theo barely stepped foot inside the dining room before announcing their presence. America was his country, and he wanted to prove to the President and First Lady, as well as to Gracie, that he was a man of action and would be a major contributor in their plan to assess German activity in the United States, as Eleanor Roosevelt insisted he call 1937 America. Hearing Mrs. Roosevelt talk about the United States, he thought the fairy tale idea of *e pluribus unum* was enchanting, and in his heart, he craved to live in such a place.

"Yes, good morning in return! Forgive me, youth, young lady, and trotting dog for only being able to bow across my lap napkin and not stand in respect to you." President Roosevelt nodded with two definite head bobs toward chairs directly to the right of where he sat at the head of the table. "Relax and enjoy the breakfast the staff has prepared. You won't find better fare anywhere. Just look at the evidence provided!" The president gave three solid pats to his stomach with his large hand while the youths laughed and Mrs. Roosevelt muttered, "Really, Franklin," and grinned along with the rest.

The butler's warning that the president's presence would be brief gave Theo and Gracie the opportunity to eat and listen and not feel the need to carry the conversation. Although he spoke in truth about the delicious food, President Roosevelt took only a few bites of a pastry while he lunged into serious instruction concerning their stay at the White House.

"I have been briefed on your passion for right. My wife tells me she has had good word and good conversation to verify what you have done in Germany. She is a reliable source, my Eleanor"—he reached over and gave one pat to her hand before continuing—"and keeps her nose in all that's good for the country—and good for me if the truth were to be known." A glancing smile in Mrs. Roosevelt's direction was the last of any fondness the teens saw pass between the two Roosevelts. They held their public conduct in a professional way as if they led the nation in tandem and not as a hierarchy of President and First Lady.

"I understand, Theo, that you have agreed to assist Eleanor with gleaning some information. It's a rather delicate task that requires a sophisticated level of covert operation." President Roosevelt wiped his mouth with a napkin he deposited on the table and set his eyes on Theo. "Do you still, this morning, agree to help this government gather information concerning German activity performed under the guise of a youth camp?" Before Theo had time to do more than open his lips and nod his head, the president continued. "I'll be straightforward. There will be risks. It will take a smart mind and a closed mouth to succeed. We invest our faith in you as being passionately able to do so."

Theo set down his fork and folded his hands at the base of his plate, looking directly into the eyes of Franklin D. Roosevelt. "Mr. President, I have personal reason on many levels for not only believing I can gather information but also for desiring to prevent evil infiltration on American soil."

Sitting back against his chair, the president's widened eyes gave Theo the response he had hoped. "Very well, then. Theo, I thank you for what you will do. Gracie, enjoy your time relaxing and enjoying what America has to offer a pretty young lady." He gave a quick flip of his wrist to which an attending butler had been programmed to respond.

"Oh, but, Mr. President, I want to help—"

"You'll be no help at this point, young lady. I'm afraid your genetics render you unable, but the countryside will not disappoint you."

No more was spoken as the butler wheeled the president from the room. The only sound came from Mrs. Roosevelt's fork upon the china plates and the creaking of President Roosevelt's rattan wheelchair.

Theo watched as the president was wheeled from the room. He placed his hand on Gracie's knee under the table, knowing her heart was anxious.

With a soft cough into her napkin, Mrs. Roosevelt took the lead as breakfast ended. "Theo, we'll go to the first floor where you will meet with Henry Wallace. He has stepped into a position of helping the president and me understand the German movement in America. We were informed of this undercurrent by our dear friend and confidant, Louis Howe. Unfortunately for all of us, Louis passed away last year. We have lost a friend, and we have lost a great deal of political expertise hidden from the eye of the media and public. Now Mr. Wallace works with me to discover what is taking place under our noses, threatening to weaken our nation. Listen to him, Theo. Question him. Then, when you finish your covert operation, report to me. Only me, Theo."

Eleanor Roosevelt stood and lifted the arms of her chair to push away from the table. Awkwardly watching the behavior in a formal dining room, Theo and Gracie emulated the moves of the First Lady.

"Uh, Mrs. Roosevelt. Gracie's heart has been torn by the German Reich. We have questions as to what I will do. Gracie and I both have questions. She knows better than most the importance of keeping secrets. May she attend my meeting with Mr. Wallace? Please, ma'am?" Theo spoke clearly and stood as tall as possible to impress and sway the First Lady.

"Young man, I know well the ability of a woman to hold her tongue and to be a strong power behind a man." Mrs. Roosevelt smiled and looked at Gracie. "My dear, you will not disappoint me in your desire to support Theo and to keep all you hear within your heart. If you at any time desire to discuss what you hear with anyone, be sure the *anyone* is only myself or Theo and *only* behind closed doors. If you can agree to these terms, you are most welcome and may be a help at this meeting."

"Oh, yes, Mrs. Roosevelt. I want to help, truly I do. I'll keep quiet, and I'll support Theo in all he's assigned to do." Gracie's curls moved in soft sways around her face as she looked first to Mrs. Roosevelt, then to Theo, then back to Mrs. Roosevelt again.

Just as German soil proved more than a young boy from the future could ever have guessed, the meeting ahead held a challenge against a power that Theo never knew existed on American ground.

Mission for One

Ushered to another formal room in the White House to meet another man in a suit and tie made Theo feel uncomfortable and out of place. The butler pushed open a door and stepped back, signaling Theo and Gracie to face a man who was anything but intimidating. Theo widened his grin. Looking at Henry Wallace was like looking at his own great-great-grandfather's picture tucked in the back of the family Bible. Even his comb-over hair flip was what the Marshall lineage had sported.

Theo placed his hand in the small of Gracie's back to allow her first into the room wallpapered and decorated with maps. Air scented by old charts inked with topographical drawings made Murphy sneeze into the air from where he rode in Gracie's arms. The snorting dog relaxed the tension and caused all but the butler to laugh. Theo was the first to speak.

"Wow! I've never seen a map that wasn't in my nop."

The raised eyebrows on the face of Henry Wallace were partial curiosity of what language the teenager had purloined. "Pardon me?"

Theo repeated his comment. "Oh, I was just saying, you have so many maps. Usually, I only see one map at a time in my nop because the screen is..." A nervous glance at his wrist made Theo catch the communication breakdown. "Oh! Ha! Yeah. Sorry. My omnoptic, we call it a nop for short. You know, to make fun of how everyone keeps everything in his nop..." Theo tapped his wrist. "But *nop* really means *nothing*." The heavy silence made Theo stammer. "It's a...well, a...oh, I know, it's what used to be called a cell phone." The only change in Mr. Wallace's tilted head was a blink of his eyes. "Um, you know, uh, phone, telephone." Theo glanced at Gracie, who stood with laughing eyes. Theo had forgotten the changes from the time he lived over a hundred years in the future. Again, Gracie came to his rescue.

"Mr. Wallace, Theo's always thinking of some way he can experiment with science. He dreams of someday making a telephone pass more than sound between people—maybe even pictures." Setting Murphy on the floor, she gave a quick squeeze to Theo's arm as she looped hers past the crook in his elbow. "What do you think, Mr. Wallace?"

The older man crossed his arms against his chest as he propped on a tall wooden table covered at one end with a roll of maps. "I think that would be an excellent idea! Perhaps he'll pick up where the Wizard of Menlo Park left off. I'm sure two scientific minds can create more than we can even dream is possible!" Though his speech was light in tone, the sincerity on Henry's face gave Gracie's explanation a credible response.

Theo didn't hide his confusion, but he was determined to hold his position in the conversation with Mr. Wallace. "Wizard of Menlo Park? Never heard of him."

"What? Never heard of...why of course you have. You're teasing me now, young man. Why, everyone has heard of Thomas Edison."

In an attempt to save face, Theo grinned and chuckled. "Ah, of course, I'm sure Mr. Edison will be glad to hear my scientific ideas."

"Oh, son. I'm sorry. You must not be from this area. I'm afraid to say Thomas Edison passed in the autumn of '31." Henry noticed Theo's expression from the egregious error, and he truly wanted to save the youth. "The East Coast keeps the memory of Edison so alive that it seems as if he hasn't really left us. A memorial tower has actually been erected over at Menlo Park to memorialize his discoveries and inventions. However, young man, we are more than ready for some new scientific blood to step up and carry Edison's torch, or shall I say *light bulb*, into the future." A soft chuckle from Henry Wallace and a gesture toward a desk surrounded by chairs lightened the atmosphere. "Now, how about we get to the plans that we must address before you become the next wizard of science!"

The remainder of the morning was spent with Henry Wallace giving information and instruction to Theo on a covert operation the

White House proposed. Gracie sat silently to control her emotions concerning the plan, hoping Mr. Wallace would let her be a part. She focused on memorizing words that were unfamiliar to her, places such as Camp Nordland and New Jersey, and even a word she knew from her own language, *Bund*. She was unsure what a German *Bund*, or federation, would have to do in America. She watched the words scroll in blue lights across Murphy's collar until they disappeared into the memory chip.

Shortly before lunch, a lady dressed in a plain yet expensive dress knocked on the door and entered only after Mr. Wallace opened the door so she could enter. "Theo, Gracie, meet Lorena Hickok, friend and confidant of the First Lady." Wallace gave a warm but matter-of-fact introduction.

Responding to Theo's standing as she entered the room, Lorena nodded to him but turned to Gracie. "Please pardon the interruption. I'm actually here a bit behind schedule and apologize for leaving you to endure the 'man talk' in the room today. Gracie, I'll now escort you to another room where you'll hear what is in store for you while Theo is away."

Gracie stood and interrupted. "Oh, but, Ms. Hickok, I want to be a part—"

"This is not work for you, my dear. We have other ways to see that your time is occupied. And"—the rounded lady added with a short smile—"call me Hick. It's a nickname I much prefer. Now, come along." She extended an arm toward Gracie as if calling a young child.

"Theo, I want to be with—"

This time it was Theo who interrupted by putting both hands on Gracie's shoulders and pulling her to his chest so he could kiss her forehead. "It's okay, Gracie. You'll not be left out. I'll be sure about that. For now, let's divide and conquer and prove how we can help my country."

Reluctantly, Gracie dropped her chin. Theo heard a light whimper between the soft curls framing her face. "Fine." Her voice didn't disguise her disappointment, but mentally, Gracie summed up Hick and was already scheming how to get a role in Theo's assignment.

RENDERED

Not caring who watched, Theo let his heart take the lead. Cupping the beautiful caramel toned face in his hands, he pushed back the curls and kissed Gracie's cheek. For a brief moment, his lips lingered on her skin, realizing he felt a tear trickle down. Unleashed power lay in a single tear. Theo embraced Gracie to reassure her that he would step where she could not see him but never breathe without the companionship of her soul.

Wallace and Hick watched in jealousy that they had no arms to embrace and desire them with such passion that words couldn't convey.

Intuition told Gracie to look back from the doorway and see determination on the face of the young man who willed his heart to hold every sparkle in Gracie's eyes until he returned. He knew Gracie had taught him many tricks for survival. He knew he had the muscle and mental fortitude of a young man who had shed the antics of a self-absorbed teen. He knew Gracie had her own world taken from her grasp, and he loved her. Yet, he didn't know the paths before them had twists that would change the world where they now stood.

"Miss Gracie." Hick's words didn't start a conversation and didn't prompt reply. The woman merely placed a hand on the young girl's shoulder as if to trigger a button that would propel her to another room where Mrs. Roosevelt waited.

Something about the First Lady reminded Gracie of her dear friend Nina, so far away in Germany. With an inhale of determination, she walked to the woman who stood by the window overlooking the rose garden. At first, neither spoke but both looked out over the rows and shapes of greenery that were periodically interrupted and decorated by splashes of color from emerging flowers. The beauty of the garden captured Gracie's thoughts.

"This is so pretty, it hardly seems real," Gracie spoke aloud to no one but herself.

Eleanor turned from the garden to watch the girl beside her. She let her eyes consider how the drab wool clothing and heavy boots were unable to suffocate the young lady's soft radiance. She stared at Gracie's tiny hands, rough, with erratic nails that lacked attention. *Poor girl. She doesn't complain of the rough life she has lived. She's very much a German rose that has been saved from gardens destroyed by Hitler and his Reich.* The regal woman's thoughts could only wonder about the unfortunate life of the young *Fräulein*. She looked down at her own folded hands.

"Gracie, this afternoon Hick will take you to a girls' boarding school. You are most welcome to enjoy the classes, but I imagine you'll most enjoy the atmosphere and new friendships you will make." She knew Gracie's heart was for Theo and not for staying in a place far from home, surrounded by people she neither knew nor cared to know.

"But, Mrs...." Gracie fought back tears being pushed out from swirling thoughts and emotions. "I don't know anyone. I don't fit. I don't look like other girls with their pretty clothes and"—she stammered as a visual of the *Hindenburg* crash flashed in her mind where she last saw Irene and her tiny satin slippers—"and pretty shoes. I'm just not like them."

Mrs. Roosevelt placed an index finger under the girl's dropped chin. "The future belongs to those who believe in the beauty of their dreams. No one can make you feel inferior without your consent." She winked at the eyes that sparkled through the tears. "Besides, Gracie, I believe in you. You'll have time to join Theo in adventures in his country. For now, you can create new dreams."

The First Lady spun on her heel and raised her voice. "Hick! Let's give Gracie a little time to freshen her pretty face. Be sure a few changes of clothes and proper school uniforms have been prepared for her. She will fit in most beautifully at Blair Academy. See that the chauffeur has enough gas in the car, and see that Sally in the kitchen has a tasty lunch packed even though it won't be a lengthy trip to take Gracie to Blairstown, New Jersey. We want her comfortable and taken in style." The lady in command swiveled back to face Gracie. "It's what you deserve, my dear. You're royalty in my eyes. Welcome to America."

The words of welcome were the final words spoken between Mrs. Roosevelt and Gracie, and the last Gracie would speak with any adult at 1600 Pennsylvania Avenue for quite some time.

Part II
American Youth, 1937

American Bund

THE CLOTHES THEO WORE REMINDED him that he was in a time gone by. *It's a uniform. It's a uniform. I have to look the part. Sigh. I look ridiculous. Everyone here looks weird. I better get my head in the game.* He let his eyes take a slow sweep around the grounds of bunkhouses, lake, and canvas tents. *Who wears a uniform to camp anyway?*

It was no wonder that when Theo and Gracie arrived in America, they were pegged as youth who matched the slogan, "Stand today for the freedoms of tomorrow." Letters from Jahile Möeller and *The Watch* in Germany had told of two kids who had proven their courage to stand against tyranny and annihilation by government. The White House briefing by Henry Wallace was as complete as could be. Warnings of suspicious bund camp activities had come to Wallace and others on the Roosevelt staff from newspaper reporters and leery legalists. He knew what people guessed. That was all. In reality, he knew very little.

Red flags of suspicion had been raised when popular summer camps for boys and girls came with a high price of entry and a regulation that the campers be children of German immigrants who had become American citizens. The American boy named Theo could help the White House discern truth from fiction by infiltrating an American bund camp.

Theo expected flag salutes and arm salutes to a German flag and führer. He expected even a little training in the German language. Never, however, did he expect a military-style training that indoctrinated young American boys to be loyal to a country and führer they did not know and turn their backs on a government that welcomed their families to Ellis Island with open arms.

Boys yelled back and forth in horseplay and nervous unfamiliarity to the new camp where they carried duffel bags filled with pants, shorts, and shirts all the same color of drab khaki green. Baggy wool socks hung exposed at the bottom of pant legs—too short by the end of summer when growth spurts would hurl the teenage boys closer to manhood. This was the summer when their thoughts would be changed, brainwashed if needed, from the innocence of childhood to the propaganda poured as the elixir of life, forming passion and goal. Theo gave his shoulders a shake. The comfortable feel of his backpack had been traded for a canvas rucksack and duffel bag. He knew, though, that safety in the camp meant looking and acting like one of the other boys. They were good boys learning a passion for Hitler's Reich and turning against the land of their birth, America.

A close observer would have noticed that the hook-and-eye fasteners that held the duffel bag closed were unhinged at one end. It wasn't in carelessness that Theo left his bag undone but rather to allow sound to penetrate the heavy canvas bag. For now, language was not a barrier breached by Murphy's translation collar. For now, Murphy's collar was recording sounds and even smells onto a memory chip to verify all Theo would report back to the White House.

"Boy! Hey, boy!" a voice shouted behind Theo accompanied by a rough shove on his shoulder. "Whazza matter, deaf boy? Can't you hear me? I see you have some kinda hearing thing in your ear."

Theo sucked in his lip to hold back words that would come out wrong. He hated bullies, but more than that, he hated bullies who thought they could pick on someone because of a perceived weakness. His back stiffened. He turned to look at the leader of the boys who stood sniggering behind him. He was tempted to pull the earbud from his ear, but then he realized if it looked like he had a weak ear, maybe this rude boy would leave him alone.

"Sorry." Theo focused on relaxing his jaw. The kid behind him met him inch for inch in height. A year ago, the bully would have outweighed Theo, but after a year of growth, he sized up the biceps of the rude boy and knew the crude talk was more than muscle strength could defend. "My ears are weak. Would you like to see if you can match the strength of my punches?" Theo stood his ground with a smirk and a tight fist around the handle of his duffel bag.

A unified voice of oohs and guffaws from the other boys heckled their friend until he couldn't back down from the challenge.

Without turning his back to the rude boy, Theo kept eye contact in a "dare me" stare as he slowly bent his knees, gently setting his duffel and rucksack on the ground. Both hands were free and fisted when he came up with a lunge forward and an uppercut to the boy's chin. For the first time since seventh grade he initiated blows, and it felt good to him, not for the sake of fighting but for the sake of standing against arrogant bullying, whether stupid boy or political leader.

It wasn't until both boys' faces were bruised and bloodied and both boys' chests were heaving that the rude boy refused to get up. Systematically, Theo wiped his brow and reached an open palm down to help the defeated boy to his feet. Emotionless, he walked over to grip the handle and strap of his bags then to the ring of onlookers where his earbud had been knocked to the ground. As he reached for the earbud, he noticed it lay beside a large boot. Standing and wiping the earbud against his heavy cotton pants, he stood full height, coming eye to eye with a man too old to be a camper. A smirk lay against the camp director's otherwise stoic face.

"Hope you enjoyed the show." Theo released his thoughts into the man's face before he turned, replaced the earbud into his ear, and walked away.

The director's eyes never left the back of Theo's head as the smirk morphed into a command. "Boys, find your tent barracks. All campers meet in the mess hall at eight hundred sharp. Dismissed!"

"Are you"—a small framed blond boy scooted around to Theo's side of the cot where the ear had no earbud—"Are you from Andover?"

"What? Where?"

"Do you, does your family, I mean, do you live in Andover?"

Theo flashed a brief grin at the boy. He looked no more than twelve, and his skinny arms hung from a camp shirt that sagged a size too large. "No." He knew he had to brush up on making excuses as he was so far out of time and place. "No, I'm not from New Jersey at all. And you?" He extended a hand. "I'm Theo…uh, I'm Friedrich." He inhaled, promising to blazon his camp name across his memory and keep his identity a secret.

"Oh, hi, Friedrich. I'm Orville."

"Orville, huh? Do you fly?" Theo chuckled at his own joke.

"Fly, no, oh! I get it! Like Orville Wright?" In reaction of friendliness, the small boy put his hand on Theo's shoulder. "I was glad you beat up Günter."

"You are, huh? Well, if you were my little brother, I'd tell you not to go around punching other people."

"But Günter causes problems. Most kids my age are scared to be in the washroom when he comes in. He does mean things and even makes us cry." The small boy leaned up to whisper in Theo's ear to avoid being heard.

Theo looked at the sincere face before he gave a solid pat to the young boy's shoulder. "I'll tell you a secret, Orville. It's okay to cry, but you're right in thinking it would just make Günter want to pick on more people." He looked around the bunkhouse before he looked back at his new little friend. "So tell me. Do any of the grownups stop Günter from bullying?"

"Bullying? You mean picking on and beating up other kids? No. Usually, the grownups stand and watch and…" The young boy furrowed his brow as he looked at the dirt floor.

"And what, Orville?" Theo noticed the boy's reluctant pause.

The blue eyes looked up at Theo. "They like it. The grownups smile, cross their arms, and watch the fights. They don't stop any fighting. They like it. Worse. They like Günter."

Again Theo put his hand on the young boy's shoulder, this time to give it a gentle squeeze. "Orville, you keep with your friends and avoid Günter's path as much as possible. I'll keep my ears open and come to your rescue when you need me." Theo intentionally tapped his earbud and grinned at the boy. "I'll tell you something else. It might be best if you act like you don't know me. I have a feeling ol'

Günter may be on my tail for some revenge, so let's not give him a reason to pick on anyone else."

"I'm not scared if you're around." The boy sat up as tall as his skinny back would reach.

Theo chuckled. "Well, let's have a code word, Orville. If I think there's gonna be trouble, I'll say, 'fly.' Then, you'll know to hightail it outa there. For now, I'm hungry. We better not be late to the mess hall. Go on now, Orville."

Without a word, the young grinning boy scampered back to his own bunk where he joined a group of twelve-year-olds who were scuffling toward the mess hall.

Theo leaned over to look into the duffel under some clothes that were not camp uniform. Blue lights were flashing from Murphy's collar. "Did you get that, Murph? Not exactly the start to camp that I had expected. I guess every time I fall into a group of kids I won't find a new friend like Yari and the boxcar children in Germany. I had just hoped it would be a little time before I came face-to-face with another mean devil. Strange place, this camp. It's not like the concentration camp where I first landed after the time jump, but I have a feeling this place somehow destroys kids too. My gut tells me this isn't the good ol' YMCA."

He reached into his duffel and pretended to be searching for a lost item as he gave a good belly scratch to the dog who had stretched from end to end of the bag, enjoying the blanket of clothing. "You're a clown, Murphy. I can't take you to dinner, but I've got to figure ways I can keep you with me sometimes. If you hear anybody, remember to ball up. For now, don't snore too loudly."

Theo was sure he heard a snort as the clasps were fastened and the duffel was shoved farther under the canvas cot bunk.

Camp Norland

LARGE SPOONS HITTING AGAINST THE rim of the large pot of oatmeal and hitting against the tray of scrambled eggs could scarcely be heard above the clamor of voices anxious for the first full day of summer bund camp. Theo chatted with boys before and after him in the food line just as most boys in the mess hall talked of everything and nothing. He held his tray and turned from the food line to look at the rows of wooden tables and benches. A grin fell from his memory.

Five years ago, he had attended a scout camp where boys and girls filed into the breakfast hall, sat at tables and chairs formed from recycled materials and reached into a continuously moving conveyor belt to pick and choose from prepackaged pastes that had flavors such as bacon, waffle and syrup, and even sausage. He was used to camps where the day's activities would be holographed onto all four walls so all could see. Activities usually involved a comfortable chair and a monitor suspended from the ceiling where it provided virtual simulations. Kids at camp in the middle of the twenty-first century didn't wear uniforms or worry about being too hot or too cold. All rooms were programmed for a constant and comfortable temperature. Once at camp Theo remembered the kids mobbed to a door and ran outside when someone brought a horse for a demonstration. Eventually, even the horse was led into a climate-controlled arena, and the onlookers shuffled back to their event stations before the summer sun caused them to break into a sweat.

"Well, that was then. This is now." Theo smacked his lips and sauntered down the first row of tables filled with younger boys until he could weave into a second row where the campers looked more his size.

"Salt."

RENDERED

Theo turned to look at a boy across the table.

"Salt."

"Excuse me?" Theo looked at the index finger then to where it aimed past his plate. "Oh, sorry. You want this?" Theo held up a small glass bottle with a tin lid filled with holes.

"Uh, yeah. Whaddya think I was saying?" The boy changed his hand from a point to an open palm.

"Sorry. It's just that where I come from all of the food is preseasoned with flavor and additives." Theo stared at the small bottle filled with white contents as he lifted it to the open hand. For a moment, his mind shifted back to the petri dish where he made an explosive when he saved Gracie from the evils of Hadamar.

"What? You're not making sense." The camper shook the bottle over his plate of eggs and set down the saltshaker. "You okay?"

"What?" Theo glanced across the table. "Oh, yeah. Man, sorry. I just had a thought of…" He inhaled. "Sorry, but I didn't catch your name." He knew it was time to focus and enjoy the day of camp.

"Harold. Harold Ford. I live on a farm in Iowa." The boy extended a tipped hand for a handshake.

"Theo, uh!" He caught his mistake. "*The old* handshake, huh? Um. Friedrich. Nice to meetcha."

Except for the continual clanging from the kitchen and the snap of "Heil Hitler!" shouted over the plates before boys sat on benches lining the long tables, nothing happened to cause Theo alarm or to put him at ease. No one seemed to care if boys sat with arms propped on the table between body and food plate. No voice reprimanded when a boy's belch made the table erupt into laughter. No one fussed about food slopped onto the floor.

Thirty minutes into breakfast the cacophony of sounds aborted as the mess hall doors opened to the camp director and his crew. Forks dropped into the silence while boys jumped to attention with an arm pointing into the air.

"Heil Hitler!" became one voice from the camp.

Exactly one hour after the doors to the mess hall opened, boys gushed from the room as if the mess hall vomited them onto the lawn.

"Rank and order, boys!" A man with a megaphone gestured along an invisible line. "Young boys in front. Older boys in back. Alphabetical order! This is the last time the command will be given, so listen and remember!" Laughter was gone as each boy hustled and whispered to find his place in the lineup.

The camp director continued his barking. "After each meal, you will line up. If you're not here, as far as anyone cares, you're gone from camp. You'll be divided by activity. Not all activities will separate age groups. After all, if there are no young boys in each group, what will the older boys use for target practice on the rifle range?" Six men who stood facing the boys laughed at the camp director's cruel joke. Several older boys slightly grinned. All young boys had knots in their throats and tears behind their eyes not knowing if summer camp would be all their parents had promised.

Men with stern faces sauntered between the rows of the lineup, walking too closely to some, stepping on the feet of others, taunting in any way to see how many could be made a victim of ridicule. One man with a slender face stopped belly to belly with the boy standing beside Theo. Only through peripheral vision did Theo witness the man standing with his head tipped over the boy, blowing a cigarette stink of breath into his face.

"Don't close your eyes, boy. At camp you need to see everything and cringe at nothing."

The boy didn't move but kept his fists balled up beside his hips to keep his muscles tight and unflinching. Theo was pretty sure the boy didn't even take a breath until the uniformed man moved on down the line.

Whatever happened to summer camp being fun? Theo's mind churned behind his eyes focused on the head of the boy in front of him until all were released to begin their day.

Whew. One thing I learned from being on the run with The Watch—always be prepared. His thoughts urged him to pull from under his cot a canvas bag and tie it to his belt. *I'm gonna thank Fritz next time I see him.*

The canvas bag was drawn up with a cord, perhaps longer than needed to open the bag, but Theo knew extra cord could be a lifesaver in the wilderness. He cinched his belt snug but not tight. The swelling from hours of hiking could cause a headache from a tight belt. The weight of the bag gave a gentle tug to his waistband.

"I'm sure this ain't no picnic, Murph." The tall young man cradled a silver ball in his hands from where it lay inside the bag. "We've gotta remind ourselves we've probably done worse than a camp. You gotta listen but stay in a ball. This is not the time or place to have to do any explaining!" Theo spoke to the ball through the canvas bag, but in truth, he was commanding his own thoughts and actions.

Standing on a knoll at the far end of the camp, Theo under his new name Friedrich, stood expressionless. Inside the canvas bag that hung from Theo's belt no one could detect a collar alive with blue lights recording noises and voices. Without expectation or speed, he took steps in place as he turned to view the layout and sights of the camp. No maps had been provided to the campers. It was only by talk in the mess hall that Theo learned of a shooting range across the hill where a Nazi flag was raised on a pole and waved adjacent to an American flag. From this vantage point, Theo saw a banner hanging on one end of the officers' quarters. He squinted to see the words but realized he was looking at German words scrawled in large letters.

Inconspicuously, Theo slid his hand into the canvas bag hanging from his waist. There was no magic spell, but he found comfort as he wrapped his palm around the silver ball. "Zikes, Murph. I'm seeing a banner, but I don't know what it says." He glanced between the tents the campers had pitched and the building where the German banner hung. "I need Gracie here. Next time I end up in Germany, I'm going to work harder to learn the language." He sighed as his fingers tapped the ball as if Murphy could transfer thoughts and ideas through his master's fingers.

"Well, I'm supposed to gather as much information as possible. I guess that means even when I see something I don't understand. Murphy, I need to turn on your vision to record the banner. Help me out, buddy. IRIS always took care of connecting my nop to your vision when we were at home. Lotta good it does for me to be back in America when I'm still over a hundred years in the past and can't use satellite to connect with my integrated robot information system." He glanced at his wrist computer and sighed then lifted the silver ball to his chest.

"Okay, Murphy. Here's the plan." Theo spoke with his lips close to the silver ball. "When I give the command, you need to unroll and morph with vision recorder mode. I'll aim your face at the banner. Then, sorry to say, ol' boy, but after a little recording of what we see, you'll need to roll into the ball again."

Cradling the ball in both hands, Theo knew he would soon hold a small beagle. He didn't know how much time he had before he would be missed down at the camp. "Murphy, unroll."

In silent transformation, the ball opened then popped before even Theo could see the change that draped his beagle across both hands. Swiveling in a smooth rotation, Theo aimed the eyes of the dog toward the mysterious banner, then swept his vision field across the bund camp.

"That's probably good. Roll, Murphy."

"Hey!" A gruff voice hit Theo from behind. "What are you doing? Why aren't you in camp!" The voice asked questions, but Theo knew he wasn't going to have time or quick thinking to answer. He turned and swung the ball down into the canvas bag.

"Uh, sorry, sir." Theo gulped at the sight of a Nazi swastika on the arm of the camp leader's uniform. "I, uh, I wandered off the path to the washhouse and lost my bearings. I thought I could figure out where I am by coming up here." The excuse was lame, and he knew it.

"Where's the ball?" The tall man in gray-green military fatigues crossed his arms across his chest and narrowed his eyes in a glare at Theo.

"Ball? Oh, uh, yeah. Uh, it's just uh, a ball that I brought from home. You know, like a lucky charm or something." Theo tried to make his voice sound calm.

"Name, camper!" the leader barked.

RENDERED

Theo looked at the badge that showed the last name of the leader, Fritz Kuhn. "Friedrich, sir. I mean, Friedrich Wells, Leader Kuhn." Theo remembered an earlier command to call all adults *leader*. Any who called a leader by the title mister would receive latrine duty.

"Wells!" the leader barked back. "Hand over the ball. You're too old to need a toy brought from home."

"But this is my—"

"Now!" Leader Kuhn stood taller with a hand extended.

Unable to think how to respond, Theo reached into the bag and lifted the ball to his chest again. "Please, sir, I—"

"Now!" The firm voice was angry and expressed no desire to appease a camper.

Theo lay the silver ball in the leader's hands wishing his dad had included a science of mind reading when he programmed the robotic dog. *Be good, Murphy. I know you are recording, but if you slip, you and I may both be finished at this camp—in more ways than just being dismissed.*

"I'm returning to camp to begin the first class of the day. I suggest you do the same." Fritz Kuhn spun on his heels and started toward camp. Theo followed and turned off toward the camper tent area, but he noticed the leader was holding the silver ball closer to his face.

Fritz Kuhn walked into the wooden cabin where wisps of strong coffee and cigarettes filled the air. Raising a fist wrapped around a silver ball, he slung his arm forward and released the sphere to roll across a wooden table where two more leaders propped their feet.

"Been out playing croquet this morning, Fritz?" Both leaders chuckled at the offhand remark as the speaker stopped the rolling ball with the three fingers that didn't hold a cigarette. The feel of the smooth metal piqued his curiosity. "Where'd you get this? Strange metal. What is it?"

Kuhn turned from the black cast-iron stove where he filled a tin cup with coffee. "Heck if I know what metal it is. I took it from a kid who was over on the knoll at the edge of camp. It looks heavier than it is. Must be hollow, but I thumped it with my finger. Sounds solid." Fritz Kuhn plopped into a wooden chair and added his feet to the tabletop.

"Not that I'm opposed to oppressing these kids, but why'd you take the ball? Now we'll have some snot-nosed kid crying for his mommy at night." The silent leader chimed in.

"No. This was a big tall kid. Too old to be playing with a ball." Kuhn sipped his too-hot coffee.

"A kid who's been here before?"

"Naw. I don't recognize him. He was that new kid who beat up Günter. I've seen him in the mess hall. I think he's paranoid about something. He's always looking around like he's always watching even when he's putting food in his mouth."

The leader named Dan sat forward, putting his feet on the floor. "Where's he from?"

"Who knows. Probably some farm in Kansas. Those farm boys have strong families and grow to have a lot of mental and physical strength. They're always on the lookout for people who want to disrupt what they call *the American way*. They grow their roots deep and are hard to push around." Fritz looked at the other two and grinned. "He's probably one of them. Maybe we'll just have to see what he's made of."

"Don't be paranoid, Kuhn! You know some of our best kids come from those German settlements in Western Kansas. They've got the brawn and we've got the brainwashing."

All three chuckled with their abuse of leadership power. The first to rise tapped Kuhn on the shoulder as he walked past. "Well, as they say in Kansas, 'up and at 'em boys.' We have a full day planned. Let's squeeze every minute of daylight and bring the boys in for a late meal."

All three leaders crammed last-minute notes, whistles, and canteens into their day packs before heading out the door. Last to leave the cabin, Fritz Kuhn reached to the center of the table to extinguish the kerosene lantern but pulled back his hand when he noticed the silver ball was missing. He took a swift turn in place and spoke to the air. "Dan, ol' boy. You probably have some trick up your sleeve. I wonder what you've done with that stupid ball." Reaching again for

RENDERED

the knob on the side of the lantern, he quenched the light leaving the cabin filled with dusky daylight as he grabbed his rucksack from the chair by the table. Heaving the straps of the pack across both shoulders, the leader of the bund camp never felt the added weight of a silver ball that had purposely, yet inconspicuously, rolled off the table and into the pack.

Training Grounds

THE CONTRAST BETWEEN SUPERVISED AND unsupervised time at the bund camp was the contrast between calm and brewing storm. For Theo, all time was agitated. Over and over, he mentally repeated his new name, *Friedrich*, given by Henry Wallace before he left the grounds of the White House. Mr. Wallace had asked by what surname he wished to be called. Feeling a common ground with the time-travel writer H. G. Wells, Theo chose the same surname.

He worried that he would forget to act in homage to a führer whom the camp hailed at mealtime with a salute. At no other time of day did the name Hitler cross the lips of the boys. Yet the German flag was posted beside the American flag that sagged where it hung in the training room as if it were sad to never hear an American salute or pledge in its honor.

Most of Theo's agitation came from not having Murphy with him. After camp director Kuhn had taken the silver ball, Theo lost his dependence on Murphy's internal recording system. He was forced to remember and to relay back to the White House sounds and words that intimated German propaganda and brainwashing.

Theo laid his head back on his pillow, too tired to care that his dirty socks were drizzling sand on the camp-issued wool blanket. *I need to get Murphy back.* Most of the past five days, he had been surrounded by other teens but isolated from friendship.

Over the week at Camp Nordland, breakfast in the mess hall had been a time when he actually enjoyed some of the other boys of the camp. With the exception of his bunk mate, Orville, and a few of Orville's young friends, his table had become a refuge for other camp fledglings around his age who had missed coming to camp in their early teenage years. So laughter flowed easily, and talk had no need to be guarded. Three times in the first week, Günter had purposely walked past the newbie end of the row of tables and had spilled some portion of his tray where it would splatter, if not directly dump on one of the first-year campers. This morning had been no different, except that Günter's target was the top of Orville's head. In a reaction as if defending a younger brother, Theo stood and went face-to-face with the bully.

"That's enough." Words came before Theo could plan a verbal diatribe.

A demonic grin broke across Günter's face. "Enough? What's enough? Did I dump enough food on the little shrimp? I have more. Maybe I should make sure that's enough." The corner of Günter's tray dumped again, this time sending both bowl and porridge down the back of Orville. His cronies laughed where they sat at their table at the other end of the row.

"I said enough. Are you so insecure that you have to pick on the young kids? Why don't you man up and face someone your own age?" The grin on Günter's face was beginning to form into a grimace that exploded when Theo added, "Or are you too scared?"

Before Theo could check his thoughts, Günter's tray hit flat against his chest. A fist followed a shove from Theo's other arm, prompting both boys to fight again, this time knocking against the wooden tables and benches that were less forgiving than the dirt of the circle where they first fought. Sounds of tin plates and cups being knocked to the floor and a quickly forming ring of boys brought the excitement to a frenzied state. Fists flew and insecurities that had been held inside the newbies found courage from the big kid named Friedrich, and the circle of watchers became a melee of fighting.

Whistles blowing and arms pulling boys apart didn't penetrate the fight between Theo and Günter until a large palm of a hand planted against Theo's forehead and pushed him backward, forcing his back and head to slam into a table. With a bloody nose and bruised face, Theo looked through the fingers of the palm covering his face into the reddened face of Fritz Kuhn. The palm raised, and Theo knew to lay still.

"Get up. Roll call is in fifteen minutes." Kuhn and the other leaders backed away from boys scattered in awkward positions where their fights had been suspended. The camp director looked around the room then stopped his glare at Theo. "Congratulate yourself, Wells! You've given all units of the camp a ten-mile hike today." Boys too scared of authority knew not to let a protest come through their lips. Kuhn scanned the mess hall again and added, "Oh, and I hope you can pee on the run because the hike will be in camp fatigues and packs and run its course in an hour. Happy hiking, boys. Clean up this mess."

Boys crawled back into standing positions, gathering plates and cups that were taken to the washracks. Intentionally, Theo stood over Günter, refusing to pick up any of the contents of the tray his nemesis had used to start the fight. In a maverick gesture, he draped a long arm across Orville's shoulder. "C'mon. They can finish what they started"—he looked over his shoulder directly into Günter's eyes—"if they're man enough."

He guided a smiling Orville out the door. "We better get cleaned up or we'll be hiking in clothes that stink before we ever have time to sweat in them." Both big and little jogged to the large tent to change and get back early to roll call.

During the running hike, Theo felt a little guilty for the punishment all had to pay for his stand against a bully, but it was evident that though they were teens, most of the youths had a pure innocence that didn't desire retribution. *These are the good boys that the Reich will brainwash. These are the Americans who are too trusting and will misunderstand an evil seeping into the veins of a democracy with arms wide open.*

Only the cronies of Günter, or those too scared to stand against him, held Theo responsible for their punishing hike. Most looped fingers around the arm straps of their packs and kept a cadence of trot instead of the usual talk that accompanied most hikes. Theo missed the extra bounce against his back of his robotic dog. Thoughts of Murphy reminded Theo of his reason for being at the camp. *If Murphy can't be here to record what's happening, I better step it up* as a spy. A quick look to both sides, and Theo realized the closest camp leaders were Fritz Kuhn and the one called Leader Dan.

Figures. Well, what's that old saying about attracting more bees with honey than vinegar? Here goes.

Without being noticed, Theo wove his jog to the edge of the mass of boys until he was positioned near but not directly behind the two leaders. He intended somehow to convince them that he was the kind of kid to be at the camp, but he had no idea what to do. The real problem was that he didn't know what kind of kid they wanted. These leaders were not the usual camp fare who stopped fights and encouraged the boys with fun challenges. They seemed to be angry and determined to demean the boys at all costs.

Okay, Theo, buck it up. These guys can't hold a candle to a jaeger, so stand a little taller and fight a little smarter. The eighteen-year-old panted in rhythm with his jog as his thoughts began to settle. *All I have to do is schmooze with these old geezers. Something will happen, and I'll step in to impress. Something. I don't have a clue what, but something.*

The cadence of the running group encouraged the boys who listened to the sounds of their boots hitting the dirt. In almost a competition-like attitude, only the younger boys let each panting breath be heard. Theo focused on the larger rucksacks strapped to the backs of the leaders who ran in front of him. *You old men gotta show your stuff, huh? You guys are probably fifteen years older than we are, but you can run with a bigger pack on your back. Well, I'm not jealous. Knock yourselves out, guys.* Theo grinned with his thoughts, letting his eyes move from pack to pack as a way to pass the time and the distance of the road.

Cadence. Yeah. Maybe that's what we need to get these campers in a better mood. Theo whipped his head left and right, taking in the faces beside him on either side. A syncopated chant bellowed from Theo's lungs.

"Gotta take a hike today…"

At first, Theo chanted then repeated himself until a couple boys joined in on the chant. After a few chants, the troops echoed back.

"Gonna make it all the way."

"Keep the pace and keep the beat."
"Let me hear your pounding feet."
"Left…left…left, right, left."
"Left…left…don't get left."
"Follow Leader Kuhn's command."
"Arm salute and take a stand."
"Camp Nordland will teach us well."
"All the rest can go…"

The chant was lost as Theo's eyes bugged at the sight of a dog's snout popping from the rucksack on Leader Kuhn's back. "Roll!" Theo yelled above the sounds of chants and foot stomps on the solid path.

"Roll!" Unthinking and unquestioning, the campers of Bund Camp Nordland chanted Theo's command to a dog who had for a moment heard his master's voice and unrolled from the shape of a silver sphere.

Confused chuckles mixed with the stomping feet before Günter picked up the cadence and the temporary position of leader.

"Left…left…left, right, left."
"Left…left…don't get left."

Without breaking their strides, Kuhn and Dan turned toward each other in a half-turn to look behind at the tall youth who had given a strange and out-of-cadence yell. Both men swiveled back to face the path ahead of them, giving each other a leery look as their eyes met in turning.

Theo was relieved that Günter took over the cadence. He knew he had to watch the rucksack without being obvious. He could hear his breathing come out heavier with the close call of Murphy blowing his cover. Mumbling the chant Günter called, Theo mentally willed his robotic dog to stay rolled as an innocent ball.

By the end of the ten-mile hike, chanting and encouragement had evaporated from the sweat and exhaustion that were consuming the bodies of the young boys. They had an unspoken gnawing at the back of their minds telling them to enjoy the camp and please their parents by becoming boys proud of German roots. But physical exhaustion chewed at the unfairness of the hike that was turned from exploration and fun into punishment. Hearts had sunk into a vice of unfair consequences, and adrenaline morphed into anger.

Though one of the older and more physically fit, Günter looked for blame as a personal way to win support from campers and convince the leaders that he was the boy who should be held up as an example to the others.

Boarding School

Despicably ungrateful. Gracie looked at the manicured lawn, old leafy trees, and pristine flower beds that added color to the stately red brick building that rose up out of the lawn. She held her breath to hold back the burning that threatened to burst from her swollen eyes. *I'm safe here. No one knows me, but everyone smiles. Look at me in this stupid skirt. How can girls stand these tight lace-up shoes? My legs look like sticks. Theo's gone. But I'm safe here.* Her thoughts momentarily stopped. She tipped her head back and felt the long curls sway against the crisp blouse on her back. *Even the sun feels good. I hate it here. Call me ungrateful. I don't care. I hate it here.* Gracie's head suddenly tipped forward in time for a tear to bounce off her hands folded across her lap.

"You okay?"

Gracie squeezed her eyes tighter and willed the intruding voice to go away. "Fine."

There was not another sound, but Gracie noticed a crisp smell of freshness that didn't go away. Keeping her head hanging face downward, she allowed her eyelids to open just enough to see her skirt and another skirt that had sat down beside her. Again, her eyes squeezed shut. *Go away. Go away. Go away.*

No sound interrupted her thoughts, but no matter the thoughts of her heart, the fresh smell did not go away—not in a second, not in a minute, not in a waft of wind that tousled the curls hanging forward from her face.

Nearly ten minutes passed before a soft sneeze came quickly and sharply from the skirted intruder sitting beside Gracie.

"Gesundheit." The blessing came from Gracie's mouth before she could stop her automatic response. *Ugh!*

"Thank you," the delicate voice spoke just above a whisper. The same soft voice that asked the initial intruding question spoke again. Then again, both sitters were covered in silence.

A soft rustling of a tissue and a soft nose blow distracted Gracie from her silence. Without lifting her head, she turned her face to see a girl sitting beside her. The girl made no attempt to look at Gracie. She just sat on the grass and leaned back on her arms. Gracie looked up enough to study the girl's profile and mentally dare her to make eye contact. Yet the girl did not. She had a soft, almost-smiling expression on her face as she soaked in the early summer warmth and watched far-off activity of the campus.

About my age. Pretty, long blonde hair. Even her face is pretty. What joke does she think she's playing by sitting here. Gracie pulled her bare legs up under her pleated skirt. "So"—she paused more from wondering what to say next than for any other reason—"so, why are you bugging me?"

The stranger turned to look directly at Gracie and smiled as if she had known her for a long time. "You've got a great place to soak up the sun. I hope you don't mind my sharing this pretty place with you."

"Who decided I'm sharing it?" Gracie snapped back, guarding any way for the girl to belittle her.

No answer came, but the pretty girl dropped her face to stare at her shoes at the end of her legs stretched out on the lawn. Gracie's eyes followed the direction of her stare. *If this girl is wearing satin slippers, I'm gonna scream!*

Gracie saw that the silent girl had the same brown laced shoes that every girl wore with her pleated skirt and white blouse uniform. Without reason she had hurt the girl, just as she had hurt another girl who just wanted to be friends before her life ended with the crash of the *Hindenburg*. The pain of hearing her own abusive voice detonated a fiery ball of emotions that had been building since she landed in America. Pulling her knees up under her folded arms, she cradled her forehead on her arms and whispered, "I'm sorry. So, so sorry."

The girl turned to kneel beside Gracie and to hold her with both arms but not to stop the cry that was evidence of a broken heart.

Mealtime came with training of how to set a table, how to hold a fork, and how to pull the food from the fork with a closed mouth. Even the proper way to sit in a chair was practiced until Gracie was sure her back would break from sitting too tall without touching the back of the chair. After dinner, more parlor lectures of sitting and standing and shaking hands stretched her nerves until she was sure she had missed the academic school and had been sent straight to a penitentiary. She finally smiled when the entire room of girls cheered at being released from their charm studies for an hour of unpacking and settling into their rooms before quiet time was enforced for the night.

"What am I supposed to do with all these clothes? Hick must have planned for me to be here the rest of my life." Gracie half-heartedly hung a wrinkled blouse across each arm. "Aha! Angel wings. Now all I have to do is fly out of here!" She swung her arms and twirled, happy to be moving and not sitting in another lecture. "Now, all I need is a window." She stared at the pale blue wall at the head of her bed. "One window. All I need is one—"

"Excuse me." A woman's voice and a knock on the open door interrupted. "Excuse me, Gracie Cooper?"

Gracie dropped her arms and turned around so fast the blouse wings fell to the floor. "Yes. I'm Gracie Cooper. I'm sorry. I didn't mean to wrinkle the blouses. I was just tired of sitting is all." She bent to scoop up the clothing. "If I'm in trouble, I'm sorry. I didn't mean to—"

"Gracie." The woman stepped into the room and took the blouses from Gracie's arm. "No, no, dear. You're not in trouble." She put a hand on Gracie's arm and spoke with a lilting tone. "Please, dear, there's no trouble, and I didn't mean to alarm you. Most girls have roommates. Yours won't arrive until tomorrow. However, there has been a request to move you to another room."

"Why? What have I done? I'm not even unpacked. I don't even know what to do with all these clothes. I promise I'll be—"

A soft chuckle from the woman caught Gracie's attention. "We start rather strictly, but really we'll loosen the strings of learning in a couple days and put all of you girls more at ease. It's no wonder you've been requested. You do seem to have a special way about you."

"Requested? What does that mean? Did Hick tell me something to do that I've forgotten?" Shaking her head, Gracie couldn't think what she had missed.

"Well, the request didn't come from Ms. Lorena Hickok. It came from Klara."

"Who?" Gracie didn't try to hide her confusion.

"Klara. I suppose she's one of your new friends. Klara's an orphan from upstate New York."

"I don't know any...orphan...? What kind of teasing are..."

"She said you met on the hillside lawn today. It's unusual to grant a student's request for a roommate unless a parent backs the request with a substantial donation to Blair Academy." The woman turned as she was speaking, looking around the room almost as if she were talking to herself. "Perhaps I'm mistaken. I'll go back and—"

Lawn? New friend? I don't know...nice to me. "No! I mean yes! Yes, I had just forgotten her name. Yes. She wants to room with me? I don't know where she is, but..." Gracie moved in little spurts of energy as she grabbed more clothes and her duffel from under the bed.

Blinking her eyes and shaking her head, the woman smiled. "Well, okay then. Here, I'll help you." She could almost feel Gracie's renewed energy as she moved about the room. In a matter of minutes she was escorting Gracie Cooper up the hall and up the stairs to a room on the third floor where the girl from the lawn stood anxiously waiting in the doorway.

"All right, girls! I'll do the paperwork tonight to move Gracie to this room. For now, tidy your things and your room. I'm afraid you still have lights-out at nine thirty like the rest of the girls. It's important to get your beauty rest. We'll have a busy day tomorrow, and the wake-up bell will chime at 5:00 AM. Good night!" Without waiting for a response, the woman pulled the door closed and left two teenage girls staring at each other, one holding a duffel exploding with clothes.

"Gracie."

"What?"

"That's your name. Gracie. I didn't know before."

"And you're Klara."

The girl from the lawn nodded.

"So, if you didn't know my name, how did you tell the lady you wanted me for a roommate? And why did you ask for me? She said orphan. Are you an orphan? Why did she agree to move me? What did—"

"Wait!" the girl shouted so loudly. Gracie's eyes opened big with surprise. "Sorry. Didn't mean to interrupt. You're asking so many questions. I was afraid I'd forget which ones to answer." She swiveled and pointed to a striped mattress. "And that's your bed. I hope you don't mind sleeping by the window."

Gracie tossed her duffel on the bare mattress, and both girls fell across their beds laughing at nothing and everything.

Small talk propelled the girls as they hung up Gracie's clothes and shuffled up the hall to the shared washroom. It seemed only minutes until the five-minute bell sounded, giving fair warning that lights would be out and all would be silent for the night.

Klara looped her arms through the metal tubes of her headboard and lifted. "Just as I thought! These beds are light enough. If you pick up one end and I pick up the other, we can put the heads of our beds together. We'll put your feet by the window, unless you think the moon may keep you awake."

"Are you kidding me! I'd love to be able to look out the window while I'm lying in bed. I guess with the heads of our beds together we'll have more space in the room." Gracie pulled open the curtain and looked out on a moonless night.

"More space? Well, sure, but that's not why we should put our beds together." Klara stood with her arms crossed.

"It's not?"

"No, silly. It's so we can stay up late and talk all night if we want to." Klara leaned toward Gracie and spoke with a whisper.

"But I thought we are supposed to sleep when they sound the 'lights-out' bell." Gracie looked at Klara with sincere innocence.

"Of course, that's what we're *supposed* to do."

Gracie reached for the foot of Klara's bed. "We better get these moved. I think I like your style."

By the time the bell sounded and lights went out, both girls were lying in their beds looking up at the ceiling and whispering.

"So, Klara, how'd you know my name?"

"I didn't."

The answer confused Gracie. "So how'd that lady know you wanted me for a roommate?"

Klara rose on one elbow, trying to see her roommate in the darkness. "Well, maybe you haven't noticed, but I'm pretty sure you're the only girl on this campus who looks like you do."

"What does that mean? Am I ugly or something?" Gracie's whisper came back with a sharp sound.

"No, silly." Klara fell back down on her mattress and covered her giggles with her blanket. "You're the prettiest girl here. No one else has such pretty skin. Your skin is soft brown. Everyone here is jealous."

"Jealous!"

"Shhhh!" Klara continued to giggle. "Jealous in a great way. You're so pretty, and your hair is so pretty. I just told my floor director that I was lonely and no one cared or understood except my friend with the caramel-colored skin, so I needed you for a roommate."

In the darkness, Gracie selfishly wished to hear Klara's words play over and over in her mind. It was so nice to be wanted here in America when the same skin made her a victim of Hitler's Reich. "Klara, are your parents rich?"

The giggles stopped from the other bed, and silence fell heavy on Gracie's ears. "Klara? Are you asleep?"

"No. I'm here. I don't know if my parents are rich. I don't even know my parents. I've lived in an orphanage as long as I can remember. When I was a baby, I should have been put on a train and sent out West where a family would have adopted me, but the paperwork got mixed up, and I got left behind in an orphanage."

"Why don't you go out West now?" Gracie didn't know where "out West" was, but she was sure it would have made Klara happier than she sounded now.

"They don't run orphan trains anymore. Besides, who wants a teenager?"

"My guardian." Gracie's thoughts reminded her of a time when Papa asked Jahile Möeller to care for her, how she rebelled and pushed him away, and how he rescued her and cared for her regardless of how she treated him. She was reminded how she loved and missed her guardian. She tried to describe her new friend who wore a silly piece of metal called a driftboard around his neck. She whispered that secretly she wished he would someday let her wear the driftboard necklace. She told of a dog named Murphy who had won her heart.

Words between the girls became fewer and fewer as the night settled. Two sleepy teenage girls told of their worlds without parents and admired the path the other had traveled until both met at Blair Academy. One was named Klara from a home for children. The director recognized intelligence and free spirit were stifled within the orphanage walls and so procured government funds to send her to a boarding school. The other was an immigrant from Germany, a street urchin nicknamed Lil' Grey, a girl who called out in her sleep for someone named Theo.

Mapmaker

GRACIE LAY ACROSS HER BED and watched the layers of clouds outside her window.

"So what are those clouds saying to you?" Klara scooted beside Gracie on the bed.

"What?" Gracie's eyes were locked on the clouds' silent, synchronized dance.

"Well, you have a very serious look on your face. Your forehead is wrinkled like you're trying to listen and think at the same time. I just called your name twice, but I think it's the clouds. Are they talking to you?"

Gracie turned toward Klara long enough for a smile to escape from her sad heart.

"Sure. They're talking." A brief pause turned her voice into a whisper. "And laughing."

"Why, what are they saying?" Klara sat up and put her folded arms against the windowsill at the foot of the bed. "Why should they laugh?"

"They're telling me where they're going."

Klara dropped her chin to rest on her arms. "I think I hear them too."

"They laugh"—Gracie paused—"like happy giggles."

"Why are they giggling, Gracie?"

"Because they're going home."

The air, filled with a powdery scent, hung silently.

"Klara," Gracie's voice broke the silence. "If you were a cloud, where would home be for you?"

"I don't know." Without looking at her friend, Klara returned the thought. "If you were a cloud, where would be home for you?"

Gracie rolled to her side. "I don't think it would be a place like a city or a country. It would be in someone's arms."

The chimes from the bell tower announced breakfast and came as an unwelcome intruder into the girls' room. Neither spoke as both Gracie and Klara stood, smoothed their skirts, looped arms into satchels, and moved into the day's activities.

"Put down your pencil!" The snap of a ruler across Miss Foster's desk punctuated the command.

Gracie's eyes flicked up from her desk into the stare of a teacher with blazing eyes. There was no doubt Miss Foster spoke to her, but the pencil froze in her hand. The finger pointing at Gracie's desk came into view.

"I'm…uh…I'm sorry, but uh," Gracie stammered scarcely above a whisper. She was mortified to have attention drawn to her.

"Put down your pencil!" again the firm voice penetrated the thick silence. "Your doodling is a distraction and shows disrespect for my lecture."

Gracie tried to loosen her grip on the pencil, but she had been caught by surprise and was sure if she relaxed she would burst into tears. "I'm not trying to disrespect you or your lecture. I'm afraid I don't know your word, uh, *dooting*."

Waves of stifled laughter crept up the aisles, washing over her with humiliation.

"Enough!" The word snapped with the ruler snapping Miss Foster's desk again.

Gracie dropped her head, letting the pencil drop from her hand and fall until it rolled to a stop on the wooden slats of the floor. The clack of shoe heels grew louder. Gracie could smell the young teacher's powder where she stopped beside her desk.

"Doodling! You understand—scribbling, nonsensical drawing. Call it what you want. It's a distraction!" Miss Foster's tight voice was loud enough for all the girls in class to hear.

"I'm so sorry, Miss Foster." Gracie bit her lower lip to force control. She kept her eyes focused on her paper. "I didn't intend to distract. I was just…" A shaky inhale made her voice quiver. "I was just drawing the lesson you were giving. I thought it would help me remember your lesson."

"Drawing? What do you mean drawing the lesson?" Miss Foster's voice eased its intensity. "Let me see your paper."

Gracie looked up at the young woman. The teacher's eyes sparkled, and her soft skin belied her firm voice. She knew every girl in the classroom was waiting to see what would happen.

A slender hand hovered over Gracie's desk. "Let me see it."

Gracie used both hands to lift the drawing as if it were a fragile piece of artwork. She laid it across Miss Foster's open palm.

A muffled cough was the only sound that breached the silence as Miss Foster examined the paper.

"This is very good, Gracie." The teacher set the drawing on the desk without moving her hand away. "You have drawn a map that follows my geography lesson of this area of the United States." She paused briefly before she pulled her index finger across the map and down where it stopped on a circle. "I recognize these states, Gracie, but what is this circle under New Jersey?"

Gracie's eyes moved from the map to Miss Foster's face. "It's where my friends Amelia and Eleanor, uh, I mean Ms. Earhart and Mrs. Roosevelt are waiting for me to—"

Gracie's words were blunted by uncontrolled laughter across the classroom.

"Girls!" With a single word and glance over her shoulder, Miss Foster silenced the room. "Your friends?"

"Yes."

"I see," Miss Foster tapped the map with an index finger. "Where did you learn to draw maps? The detail follows my lecture notes, and you have proportioned the map very well. Do you draw for hobby?"

Gracie knew the other girls were listening, but her nervousness was better controlled if she pretended only she and the teacher were in the room. "It's a craft I learned from my papa in Germany. He is, I mean, he was a *Kartenhersteller*. You know, a mapmaker."

Nancy Foster stood looking down at the student whose head had dropped so no one could see how tightly she squeezed her eyes shut to hold back the burning tears. "A mapmaker." Her reaction broke the painful quiet of the room. "A mapmaker who taught you his craft. How endearing." The teacher's soft voice spoke only to her own mind and heart.

The young woman stooped to pick up the pencil lying beside her shoe. Without a word she put the pencil across Gracie's open palm and gave a light squeeze to her wrist. In a breeze of movement that left a soft scent lingering beside the desk, Miss Foster returned to the front of the classroom, and as if she had never stopped her lecture, resumed teaching.

It wasn't until after dinner that Klara returned to her room and saw Gracie sitting on the bed surrounded by unopened books. Gracie didn't look up, but Klara risked breaking the silence of study time and scooted across the mattress until she sat with her back against the wall beside her roommate.

"Sorry." Klara had hoped Gracie would speak first, but nearly a minute passed before she spoke.

"For what? Why should *you* be sorry?" Gracie's voice was accusatory, not really asking a question and punctuating the *you*.

"I'm sorry about what happened in geography class."

"Why? That had nothing to do with you. I can get in trouble by myself." Gracie let her angry heart fall out into the open, not caring who was hurt with her words.

"She likes you."

"Miss Foster? Like I'm going to get sucked into that lie. She only likes to make girls feel worthless. No, not girls, just girls like me."

Klara sat forward and faced Gracie. "Stop. Just stop right now."

"I don't need your pity party!" Gracie's voice showed she wasn't up for another lecture.

"This isn't a pity party!" Klara raised a raspy whisper. "Lower your voice. You want trouble? If we're caught talking during study time, we'll get to spend more time than we want in isolation. So just stop. Stop yelling and stop thinking about yourself! I didn't come to give pity. I came because I felt sorry that the girls laughed at you today." Klara wiggled off the bed and plopped into her own pile of books on her own bed.

Bell chimes to end the study period and to call the girls to dinner were the first sounds to break the silent tension in the room two hours after Klara and Gracie had fought with words.

"Gracie, may I see your geography drawing? It might help me learn Miss Foster's lesson."

Gracie gave a half huff, half chuckle as she pulled the paper off the top of the books she stacked on the corner of their shared desk. "Klara, you're not a good liar. You just want to see what caused the commotion."

"Maybe." She grinned. "I am curious." Klara looked at the map of the northeastern United States sketched from the morning's lecture. "I think this dot must be our academy." Klara's finger hovered over a penciled dot on the map. "So what's this dot?" She drew an invisible line in the air as her finger moved to the right.

"I'm not sure. I mean, I know what the dot is supposed to be, but I'm not sure if it's in the right place."

"So what is it?"

"It's a place called Andover."

Klara raised her eyebrows out of curiosity. "Oh, I think I know where that is, but I don't remember Miss Foster mentioning Andover."

"She didn't." Gracie bit her lip wondering how much to say. She wanted help finding a location, but she couldn't risk loose lips. "I have a friend there—at a camp."

"Camp? You mean Camp Nordland? The bund camp?" Klara tilted her head.

"I think so. Have you been there?" It was Gracie's turn to be curious.

"No. I'm not sure any orphans from the home even get a chance to go. I've heard it costs a lot of money, and rich kids get sent there so their folks can get them outa their hair." Her laughter encouraged Gracie to feel at ease.

"So?"

"So what?" Klara seemed to have forgotten Gracie's need.

"So, is this the right place for Camp Nordland?"

Klara wrinkled her brow and studied the map. "I think it's actually a little farther down and over." Again her finger traced an imaginary line. "Because there's a road the orphanage used to get me here, and I remember seeing the Andover sign." She looked up at Gracie. "Remember Andover from reading *The Crucible*?" Gracie's blank stare didn't interrupt Klara. "At the witch trials—you know, in the play—they talk about Andover, so when I saw the sign, I recognized the name." Klara looked as if waiting to be congratulated.

"So it's on a road?" Gracie glossed over most of Klara's words about some play she had read involving witches, trials, and Andover.

"Sure, it's the road that comes right up to the front door of our hallowed halls." Klara had lost all curiosity with the sound of the second set of chimes indicating the start of dinner. "We better get to dinner or we won't care about anything except our empty stomachs!"

As Klara swiveled and stepped to the door, a contented sigh came from Gracie's soul as she gave a soft pat to the map on her desk before she followed her helpful friend.

Elsewhere

THREE WEEKS INTO THE SEMESTER, classes at the boarding school held some of Gracie's interest, but she found little relevance for her new life in America. She was ready to feel a wisp of adventure float through her heart. Her stomach was full from the hearty breakfast, and she knew to waste time was to waste energy that she would need.

Her desk chair was the perfect ladder to reach the top shelf of the narrow closet where her heavy cotton pants had been tucked away and replaced by the traditional boarding school uniform. *Ugh, I sure didn't think I'd be excited to wear you again!* In no time the woolen skirt had been dropped and the pants pulled over her legs. *Whew! Good thing I'm leaving this place. Too many more meals of hearty oatmeal and potatoes and my belly might be strangled in the waistband!*

Gracie stuffed a couple shirts and undergarments into her satchel then checked herself and spoke into the quiet room. "Okay, Gracie. You're not just missing Theo. You're starting to act like him too!" She pulled the crumpled clothes out of the satchel. *If I roll these, I can fit more...* She smoothed and rolled each item, replacing each into the bottom of the bag. *No room for my coat...summer, don't need it anyway.* She looked around the room and tossed her coat under the metal bed. *Probably best if I don't look like a girl.* She pulled a knit hat over her hair and tucked curly strands inside.

Oh! And my map. Thanks for your compliment about my map, Miss Foster. I'm glad to hear it looks kinda right. And thanks for helping me find Andover, Klara. You're a good... Gracie's thoughts were just finishing as she folded the map, gave it a kiss, and tucked it in the top of the satchel.

"Ready or not, here I come, Theo." Gracie patted the metal bed frame as she slung one strap of the satchel across a shoulder and started for the door. "I'll miss you, Klara." The cold metal doorknob sent a chill through her nerves. *What am I thinking!* Her hand pulled away as if an electrical shock had come through the knob. She turned to the window.

"Oh, Klara! Why do you have a room on the top floor?" Gracie shoved the window frame upward, letting fresh air rush into the room. "Sorry, Hicks. You'll have to tell Mrs. Roosevelt that I didn't mean to mess up this nice satchel, but I'm pretty sure it will survive the fall." Gracie wiggled from the strap and held the bag as far down the outside wall as her arm could dangle before she released it to make a muffled plop on the soft grass at the base of the building. "Too bad that won't work for me."

Back inside the room she rummaged through her closet before she pulled out four pairs of regulation cotton stockings that Hicks had added to her boarding school wardrobe. "Never quite liked wearing you itchy stockings even when the days were still cooler, but maybe you can help me escape from this prison." Stocking legs were tied together in a ropelike fashion with one end tied around the metal footboard where her bed butted against the wall under the window. Gracie tugged the stocking rope and whispered a quick prayer that she wouldn't kill herself getting to the ground. Gracie's upper torso leaned out of the open window where only rough red bricks lined the walls. She knew the stocking-rope wouldn't get her all the way to the ground, but she could jump the distance that remained.

Don't look. Don't look down. You'll just turn into a big baby. Be careful. Feet out the window first, she paused, letting her stomach rest on the windowsill as she wiped her hands on her pant legs and squeezed her fingers around the thin stocking. Starting her descent, she looked up where the stocking stretched across the sill. *Gosh. These stockings have more stretch than I realized.* She looked at the wall in front of her eyes to focus on bracing her boots against the rough brick.

Hand. Hand. Hand. Gracie mentally talked her way down. Twice, sudden jerks from the stretching stockings caught Gracie's breath, but she was unprepared when the pull against the bed frame was too much for the knot to hold. The unwound stocking gave to

Gracie's weight, letting her drop to the ground. She lay with the wind knocked out of her lungs, holding the makeshift stocking-rope that had come untied.

"Ugh. What is it with me and climbing through windows!" Gracie rolled onto her side and pulled her knees close to her stomach. One hand rubbed the back of her head where it hit the ground after her back took the brunt of the blow. "I'm pretty sure this is how I'll kill myself someday." Slowly, she rolled to her shins, letting her hair fall around her face as her forehead rested on the hard ground. *Get up. Get up. Get up.* Her mind commanded her faster than her unwilling body unwound. She reached for the cap that had come off in the fall.

"Hey!" A man's voice caught Gracie's attention. "Hey! What are you doing?"

Pivoting her forehead on the ground, Gracie turned her face enough to see a form headed her way from across the lawn.

"*Trottel!*" Gracie wasn't sure whether her German tongue was calling herself a fool or the form running toward her, but she knew this wasn't a time to explain what had just happened. Her pulse accelerated, pushing her to run. Plunging into a hedgerow bordering the campus, she squatted and looked back where her satchel, once on the ground under the dormitory window, was being lifted by the gardener who had tried to stop her.

"My map!"

Refusing to cry, she willed her breathing to slow as she wiped the dirt from her pants and began looking through the trees for a road.

"Who needs that stupid map? Klara said a road will take me to Andover. Too bad, Blair Girls' Academy. Keep my map. I don't need it!" Bolstering her heart, Gracie pulled and released a tree branch where she walked deeper into the hedgerow and away from the school campus.

Gracie's plan to leave the academy seemed easy, but fear of being caught kept her from the open roadway that ran near the trees. *Ugh. Why didn't I just walk out the front door? Why'd I have to fall so close to the gardener? Why didn't I grab my satchel? I don't dare walk on the road. I won't go back now.* With despondent resolution, she turned and stepped into the forest.

A half day of walking deepened the discouragement lodged in Gracie's heart. She feared she would lose her strength and willpower and get lost so far from anyone or anything she knew. The trees all looked the same. Even the road had twists and turns that all looked the same. After leaving the cover of the woods several miles away from the town of Blairstown, Gracie walked along the side of the road. No cars passed in the hours from afternoon to evening. Ready to find cover for the night, she turned back into the forest until she lost all sense of direction in the shades of darkness. Summer nightfall chilled her when the sun hid behind the trees of the forest, and the ground where she slept seeped dew into her canvas pants as night hours crept deeper into the dark.

The dense pile of leaves rustled, scaring a fox who ran deeper into the woods. The teen crawled from the decaying mass that had given little warmth and cover through the night. Gracie let the dancing river swim past her dangling arms until the cool mountain stream numbed her skin. She forced herself to rinse her face in the icy water. Leaves and dirt shook from the knit hat and washed away from the caramel skin. Summer was a strange time to wear a knit cap, but keeping her hair tucked under the hat made her feel more like the urchin running the streets of Germany, now more than two years since her guardian, Herr Möeller, had rescued her and given her a home. Gracie's hopefulness brightened in the morning sun.

"Okay, river. Take me to the road. I'm outa here."

Road of Reckoning

The babbling of the rolling river became a voice that smothered all other sounds as it sang to the young traveler in the forest. Over a day had passed since Gracie left the academy. She used the forest as cover in her search for Theo at a camp she only knew by its name. The forest brought both good and bad memories of the days in Germany when she and Theo ran from the evils of an asylum called Hadamar.

Gracie sat on a grassy mound where the river undercut the bank. She sang out to the river. "Here I sit on my throne! Yes, yes! Clap your hands for me! Mrs. Roosevelt called me royalty. Look at my beautiful crown!" The small-framed girl tied the ends of clover flowers together and placed a strand across her hair. Her laughter was carried across the babbling waters where a pine marten sat up on its haunches and gazed at the laughing creature.

"Oh, look at you!" Gracie pointed at the small animal that flinched at the attention and ran into the underbrush. "No! Please wait! I'm sorry! I'm not really crazy. I just need to have someone to talk to." She crawled from the mound overhanging the river and ran after the pine marten. "Okay, little guy, I'll play chase with…ugh!" In her playfulness, Gracie forgot to watch her footing and tripped when her foot slipped into a hole in the ground.

"Oww. Nice, Gracie. Real nice." She sat up and rubbed her ankle. "Where'd you go, little guy? Are you in the bushes laughing at me?" She tilted her head as she noticed a whooshing sound that came from over the hill. "Wait. What's that?" She crawled up the hill and saw a roadway that cut through the mountains.

"*Ach du meine Güte*!" Gracie's surprised cries of "oh my goodness!" were heard only by the curious pine marten as she lumbered out of the ditch and stood on the rocky shoulder of the road. Throwing her arms into the air, she shouted in a happy dance. "Have you been following the river and hiding over this ridge? Woohoo! Mr. Road, take me away to Andover!"

Gracie stared up and down the road, watching for another car to break the silence. "Well, no signs saying north, south, or too bad for you…" She tipped her head back to find the sun above the forest. "No problem, I'll just figure direction another way." She continued to look at the sky as she stepped backward toward the middle of the road. "Okay, your turn, sun. Give me a shadow so I know which way I—"

A blaring horn and screeching tires didn't stop a red sedan from skidding around the bend and into the rocky shoulder where Gracie had come from the forest. The car spun to a stop with the back end twisted and one tire against a rail that divided road from the embankment that ended at the river. Gracie's startled scream was drowned out by the car. A void hung between a teenager in the road and a driver who sat motionless with two hands still gripping the steering wheel.

The red Ford sedan glistened in the sunlight as the door opened on its new, noiseless hinges. The sole of a man's scuffed shoe crackled on the rocks. Gracie swallowed hard and watched as a well-dressed man stood and stepped away from the car. He swung the door shut, glanced at the fender that had just missed the guardrail, and spun to stare at Gracie in a fluid move that scarcely gave her time to take another breath.

"*Herr*, I'm so sorry. I was just trying to see my shadow. I'm lost and I…" Words poured from the girl, shaken and sorry.

"*Herr?*" the man interrupted. A half smile grew beneath his light-blue eyes. "Are you German?"

Gracie had reacted, never intending to raise suspicion about why a girl with a different language would be away from anyone she knew, away from any place she called home. Her mind spun as she tried to remember what she had just said and to plan what to say now. She looked at the man who had folded his arms across his chest and tilted his head. He squinted his eyes as if he was studying her face.

"I, um, I can…" Gracie stuttered through drifting thoughts. *He doesn't look old enough to be slow. If I run back to the forest… He won't leave his car to…*

"*Bist du allein?*" the man asked, "Are you alone?" in the German tongue as a trick to answer his own question.

"Yes, um, no." Gracie caught her mistake.

The man chuckled. "Well, are you or aren't you?"

"Um, yes. I was born in Germany."

A rolling laugh came forward as he stepped into the road. "Of course, but are you alone?"

"I'm alone in the road, but there are others." Gracie swung a pointing finger toward the forest.

Swiveling where he stopped in the road, the driver glanced past his car.

Now, Gracie, run. Go. Run. Thoughts begged her to escape. She ran hard, not planning, not thinking, just running. Not knowing where or even why, but with an instinct that she was running for her life. She could hear the leather soles of the dress shoes in a scraping run in the road behind her. *Help me. Someone help me. Please, God. Someone help me. Some…*

Air forced from Gracie's lungs as arms wrapped around her throwing both man and teen into the weeds at the side of the road. The man grunted and pulled Gracie's arms behind her.

"Ow! You're hurting me!"

"Not my fault! Why'd you run, you little imp!"

Gracie kicked the weeds, unable to move without pain shooting into her shoulders. "Let me up! Help! Someone help me!" Her screams were absorbed into the grass and nearby forest.

"You're a wild one, aren't you." The man jerked her to her knees without releasing pressure on her arms held behind her. "Let's try this again." At first, the man's voice became a soft singsong. "If you remember, *you* were the one standing in the road. I swerved so I wouldn't kill you. *You* caused my new car to nearly be wrecked. *You* spoke to me in German. When I tried to ask if you needed help, *you* ran! It seems to me that one of us is causing problems. Now, care to try this again?"

The man stood first, keeping a binding grip on Gracie's arms. As she pulled her legs under her to stand, her knit hat caught on his sleeve button. Long soft curls tumbled out from the hat that stretched away from her head.

"Ow!" With hands bound behind her back, Gracie tipped her head downward to keep the hat from pulling against her hair.

A dark shadow oozed from the pores of the man who stood frozen, staring at the curls that lay across his fingers that untangled and caressed the soft hair. His mind formed a vision of a girl he had trailed on his recent flight to America. His mind's eye recalled a black-and-white photo of a man, woman, and small child with curly hair, a ruined photo he left at the site of the burning *Hindenburg*. His hands tightened around the locks of hair.

"Ow! You're pulling my hair!" Gracie kicked the man's shin.

"Oh." He dropped the long curls and moved his palm against her cheek to turn her face toward his own. "Sorry." Though his voice had dropped to a whisper, it held a lilt of happiness. "Please"—he paused and let his eyes wander across her face—"please, don't run. Let me take you where you're going." He released the painful hold and softly but completely wrapped his fingers just above her elbow.

Gracie stared back at the man whose disheveled hair and crumpled clothes were proof that she could not easily escape. She looked up the road where the red sedan waited and teased that it could take her farther. "First, promise you'll not hurt me." She faced him and spoke with a voice of strength. "Promise you'll take me where I want to go."

"*Fräulein*, the miles I travel with you will someday not matter. I promise to deliver you, letting no one, neither human nor animal, interfere." With his free hand, the man gesticulated toward the car while inhaling a breath of satisfaction. "Shall we go?"

As the red sedan pulled back onto the road, Gracie sat determined not to speak but replaying the man's words that swirled unsettled in her mind. She realized the car was speeding up the road, but the man had not asked where she wanted to go.

RENDERED

"I need to see the president." Gracie looked straight ahead and pushed up with her feet to look taller in the seat.

A quick glance from the driver and the car was filled with a boisterous, loud laugh. Gracie scowled. She was sure she hadn't said anything funny, but the man's response was not what she expected. She stomped her foot against the floorboard.

"Now." Gracie didn't raise her voice, but she pushed strands of hair back under her cap to keep the man from seeing she was beginning to shake.

The laughing man grinned and looked over at his beautiful passenger. "I'm supposed to take you to the president? What president?"

Gracie looked at the man but glanced away to avoid eye contact. She spoke toward the car window. "President Roosevelt! *Dummkopf.*" She paused to mutter just loudly enough for him to hear being called a fool. "Just take me there. You said you would."

"Actually, little darling, I said I would deliver you." The man smirked and glanced in his rearview mirror, seeing they were alone on the stretch of road. "I didn't say *where* I would deliver you."

Scarcely were the words out of his mouth than his hand extended across the seat and clamped onto Gracie's arm. "You'll go where I take you, *Fräulein.*"

The man had been watching Gracie move her hand along the door beside her until her fingers wrapped around the silver door handle. He knew her heart was beginning to panic, and if she truly was Jahile Möeller's daughter, she would fight in rebellion. He wasn't wrong that she would fight.

The man slammed a foot against the brake pedal causing the car to careen as he steered with one hand and held mercilessly to her small arm as she fought to get away. The door of the red sedan swung open while the car spun to a stop in the middle of the road. Fighting for her freedom, Gracie swung her leg across to catch the man's chest with her worn and heavy boot. Angered from the kicking boot, the man muscled his strength against the kicking and doubled her over until he could bend her arm behind her with one hand and grasp the hat and a handful of hair with the other.

"All right, you little fighter. You're my prize, and I don't think you'll win this one." Pulling her by the arm wrenched behind her back, he dragged her from the sedan and cradled her neck in the crook of his other arm. Gracie was glad to feel the hard road beneath her boots though she could scarcely kick for keeping the pressure of his arm from choking her.

The powerful man fumbled with the keys to open the trunk of the sedan. Gracie frantically writhed and kicked to throw the man off-balance, but he only tightened the grip around her neck. She clawed at the arm that threatened to stop the air she gasped to breathe. A sudden squeeze of his arm was too much for the young girl's neck, and her air passage closed. In the darkness that overwhelmed her, Gracie's fighting body fell limp in his arms.

Before the trunk lid closed over the unconscious girl, Gustav Kaercher couldn't resist the urge to drag his fingers down the soft caramel-colored flesh of her arm. He lifted her hand and folded her arm against the still body.

"Sleep tight, princess. Daddy can't help you now."

Survival

"Friedrich! Hey, Friedrich! When we're done, we get to finish the evening with free time. Wanna walk to the creek with me and my friends?" The camp kitchen was small, but Theo ignored the voice as the bunkmates finished their assigned time of cleanup after dinner.

Theo slung a dish towel over the outdoor clothesline and looked down at Orville's freckled face. "Oh, sorry, bud. I guess I was lost in thought and didn't hear you." He gave a gesture toward two other young boys. "No…"

In a gesture to wave his young friend on his way, Theo's arm brushed against the metal driftboard charm dangling from the lanyard around his neck. In an instant, he smiled and pulled the lanyard over his head.

"Hey, Orville! Take my good luck charm with ya. It'll make me feel like I'm out there having fun too. You guys go on. I'm kinda tired. Plus, I have an old leg injury I need to take care of or else you'll be carrying me on the next hike." Theo tossed the lanyard with the driftboard charm to Orville, who slipped it around his neck in one motion after the catch.

Orville gave a quick laugh and jogged to his friends, waving an arm crooked backward in Theo's direction.

I wish my leg injury was a joke. Theo gave a heavy sigh. *I can almost hear IRIS, "Preventative medicine, Theo. Exercise is better when you're off the sofa."* Sheesh. *I bet she never dreamed in her little robotic brain chip that I'd spend a year without a sofa or a HoloGame.*

A paper tacked beside the door caught Theo's attention as he was leaving the mess hall.

> Advanced Wilderness Survival
> Challenge Yourself to Leader Dan's Training
> Only for Stout of Heart and Body
> Mess Hall at 0500 hours
> Bring Knife, Rope, Whistle,
> Any Other Tack You Choose.
> All Interested Sign Below

Theo lifted the pencil dangling from a string tacked to the wall. So far, only five boys had signed. It wasn't until after he signed his fake name, *Friedrich Wells*, that he noticed Günter's name scribbled three lines above his.

"All right, Günter. Let the games begin."

By lights-out, Theo's bunk was silent. He knew a full night of sleep would be necessary for whatever wilderness survival activity would be thrown at him the next day. One part of his heart wanted to tell young Orville that he would wake before most of the other campers, but another part of his heart understood that the less Orville knew, the better, maybe even safer, for the young kid.

Against the dark silhouettes of the large tents, a gentle stream of smoke pulled light from the smokestack of the wooden cabin where the camp leaders sat and planned the next day's activities. Director Kuhn pulled his rucksack from a chair and tossed it under the table so he could prop up his tired legs. The momentum of the fall helped a wiggling ball tumble the rucksack to its side. The ball rolled out of the pack, unnoticed by anyone at the table and split just enough for a small black nose to poke through the opening. Blue lights flashed inside the ball. A large foot from someone at the table scraped across the floor, knocking into the ball that sealed as it rolled and came to rest on the open floor. Nothing blocked the sound of voices that recorded on a chip inside Murphy's ball.

Fritz Kuhn started the informal meeting. "Camp seems to be progressing as usual. What are your thoughts? Are the boys learning the pledge to the führer as they should?"

"Whaddaya mean?" A second leader leaned back in his chair and linked the fingers of both hands across a bulging belly. "They seem to be standing and yelling 'Heil Hitler' at mealtimes and after language classes."

"Good for all of that, but you know me. I want to be sure these boys aren't just spewing camp chants. I want to get so far under their skin that their first reaction to everything in life ties back to Germany. I want them to suck in American air and blow out German soul." Kuhn drummed his fingers on the table. "There's no guarantee they're getting any heritage revival at home. They come to this camp for that. So, back to my question."

Leader Dan inhaled to signal that although usually quiet, he was ready to speak. "So, do I think their chant of führer loyalty is automatic? Yeah. Do you want us to kick it up a bit and have them chant more, like at—"

"No, no," Kuhn interrupted the deep voice. "No, if you think the chant is automatic enough, I'm good with that. Let's do our job, but let's not go overboard." The leader's heart pulled tighter within his chest. It was a fine line between his giving Hitler the praise while keeping the power to himself. Fritz Kuhn thrived on any recognition he received as the American führer. He'd do all within his ability to keep Hitler from having too much influence on his turf.

Dan said nothing but let a smirk hold a cigar smoldering in his teeth.

The fingers that crossed over the swollen belly jiggled as the other leader laughed. "Whazza matter, Kuhn? You afraid Hitler might get too much credit? You sure want to keep the American-Germans under your thumb, don't ya? You've been an American citizen for nearly three years, climbing the ladder of power each year, and you still act afraid that more people are going to kiss the whiskers of Hitler than bow to you. Maybe you've been smelling too many chemicals in your day job to notice, but you're doing just fine with your influence here. Bund camps are popping up all over America to keep the German heritage strong. You've already got one German Iron Cross from the Great War. Quit fighting yourself, trying to get another."

Director Kuhn turned a stoic face toward the outspoken leader. "If that's your way of supporting me, Gerhard, I'll accept it." His tight lips weakened into a slight smile. "You're right. Hitler doesn't deserve too much credit here. These immigrants are from his country, but they're not his people. They're mine." He flicked an ashy cigarette into a glass dish on the table then pushed scattered ashes toward the dish with the side of his little finger. "The kids of these camps need German influence, not just heritage. Heritage is something you set on a shelf with a picture of *Großmutter und Großvater* and all other relatives still in the mother country. Influence is something that oozes into your character until it can no longer be separated out."

The round leader nodded and grinned as he raised a rough palm into the air. "Thanks for the lesson, O mighty one. Heil Kuhn." He spoke with little energy.

"And tomorrow?" Dan spoke into the sudden quiet.

"Tomorrow. Yes." Kuhn nodded at Dan but turned to look at the leader across the table. "Gerhard, you'll stay at camp and oversee the classes and activities conducted by our teachers. Give the boys an extra hour of swim time and outdoor games. Their roughhousing will tire them. Dan, you'll be exhausting a special group of your own tomorrow."

"You make my survival training sound grueling. Don't give me so much credit," Dan sneered.

"It's time to up your game, Dan." Kuhn moved to find a more comfortable spot in the wooden chair. "These boys are feeding right into my plan. With the exception of two—a young kid and a weak kid who's only here because his father has convinced him he's sure to move up in Henry Ford's factory—you have a strong set of boys for your wilderness training. Let's see what they can do."

"What are you planning? Some kind of awards ceremony for building a fire in the woods?" Dan's sarcasm was intended to keep the tone light yet dig out more to feed his curiosity.

"Before camp started, I had a visit from Gustav Kaercher—"

This time it was Gerhard who interrupted. "Kaercher! When did he swim over from Germany?"

Kuhn raised his eyebrows. "Seems he's been tracking a couple people who made enemies of the Reich, specifically Viktor Brack."

Dan gave a low whistle. "Not one I'd want to tangle with."

"So it seems," Kuhn continued, "they came to America to escape. Kaercher was assigned to track them and get some journal that belongs to the government or Brack or something like that."

"If you don't mind my sounding like I don't care, can we get to how this all ties to my survival course? I'd like to set the plans and get some sleep tonight." Dan's interest was waning.

"Fair enough. Gustav came to me for help, wants to use two of our best kids."

Gerhard choked up a laugh. "How does he plan to play cat and mouse with a couple of our bund kids? I don't care how good they are at surviving, unless they're military trained, how are they going to fight Brack's war?"

Kuhn's stoic face looked directly at Dan. "Seems it was two kids who stole a journal from Viktor Brack. Gustav figures to beat them at their own game. He doesn't have *Hitlerjugend* on American soil, so he came to us for the next best thing. Your boys can be trained, but I suspect that they have some natural survival talents of their own. Tomorrow, I want you to spend half a day training, then turn them loose to see who survives a challenge. Put them into pairs and give them the toughest test in the woods. My guess is the two who can help Kaercher will be the top contenders."

Dan nodded as he looked at the list he had pulled from a pocket. "Looking at the names of the campers who signed up, I have a pretty good idea who's going to rise in the challenge." He tapped the paper with a finger. "You want me to put Günter and that new camper, Friedrich Wells, together?"

"No, Dan, you know as well as I do they hate each other."

"So why does that matter?"

"One-on-one we've witnessed their anger. Both look pretty determined. Put them together and they'll learn to cover each other's weakness. Let's push them to limits, make them overcome their own weaknesses. Pit them against each other. If they both come out with strong skills, you've got your two boys."

Dan stood and smothered his cigar into the ashtray. "Excuse me, men. I need to retire to the corner where I can make some adjustments in tomorrow's wilderness survival training."

The leaders' cabin fell into darkness except for a small lamp in the corner by Leader Dan's bunk.

The Gauntlet

THE MUSKY ODOR OF RAIN-DRENCHED canvas filled the large tent. The sound and heavy smell recalled images behind Theo's closed eyes that creased his face with a slight smile. He lay with his eyes shut in the bund camp tent, but his heart remembered lying under a canvas on the back of a flatbed truck that smuggled Gracie and him to a castle in Germany. His thoughts spoke to his heart.

Ah, Gracie. You told me the smell of rain-soaked canvas would be a good memory. You were right, a good memory of being with you. Don't worry, Gracie. We'll be together, soon, hopefully, very soon.

Theo ran his hand down the blanket until he could pull his wrist computer from his pocket. At the White House briefing about the camp, Henry Wallace had warned Theo not to wear the nop, even as a watch. It was too different, too advanced, too suspicious to wear. He shouldn't get caught being a spy in the form of a 1937 teenager. With the heat from his hand, the display of green numbers blinked 4:27 AM.

Ugh. Too early to be awake. Too close to morning to fall back to sleep. He inhaled deeply to pull the memory seeping from the wet canvas. *Too wonderful to have a sweet memory of Gracie. Too wet for the survival training class today. Ugh. Go figure.*

Theo slipped the nop back into his pocket unaware that a yellow light rimmed the face of the computer, alerting that someone, somewhere in a future time, was trying to contact him. He drifted back into a heavy sleep.

Restless dreams plagued the eighteen-year-old who couldn't find comfort on the narrow cot. The early morning rain brought a chill, but he kicked off the wool blanket issued to campers. In restless sleep, he ran in his dreams. At first, Theo felt no pain, but he knew his body ran over a rocky path as blood spurted from an open wound on his leg.

Two shadows passed through Theo's sleeping brain.

> *A silvery, wispy cloud floated behind him. The cloud reached for Theo. He tried to reach back for the cloud, but no matter how far he reached, the silver cloud dissipated in his touch. Swirling around the path, both in front and behind was a darkness that burned his skin and choked the breath from him as he ran. It was an impenetrable darkness—not like a night sky but a thickness that had no memory of ever holding any light.*
>
> *Theo wanted to run from the darkness, but something pulled at his entire being, and he knew he couldn't leave the silver cloud. He sensed that he must stand between the darkness and the silver cloud. The consuming stench of the darkness sucked him into its vortex until he was squeezed out the other side of the all-consuming blob. He knew the darkness wanted to separate him from the silver cloud. It did not want him. The darkness would not be satisfied until it had consumed the silver cloud.*
>
> *"Noaoah!"*

A distorted yell came out of Theo's mouth in the form of a muted and mumbled scream unheeded by the other sleepers.

It wasn't a fear of the darkness that tossed Theo's body and mind in restless sleep. It was a fear of what the darkness wanted.

> *He didn't know why the darkness wanted it, but he knew he had to fight with every fiber of his being to save the silver cloud. Turning, he saw his body punch and claw to penetrate the burning darkness and find the cloud.*

RENDERED

The darkness sliced at him with razorlike talons, separating his muscle from his bones, weakening his struggle, but months of running from the Reich in Germany had given him a muscular strength to match his determined heart.

Theo felt like his eyes bulged from his skull as he glared into the darkness to find the silver cloud. As if begging for his rescue, a wisp of silver shot through the darkness, just beyond his reach.

Before him the darkness hovered over a lake. Theo's swirling thoughts of dream knew the silver cloud lay on the other side of the water. He gulped the air, willing to trap his breath in his lungs as he dove into the water. He swam with a propulsion of courage. Just as his breath threatened to escape the lungs that held it, he exploded out of the lake.

His eyes opened into the light of the silver cloud. The vision before him renewed his strength.

He lunged with both arms extended. The silver welcomed his touch and cooled his skin burned by the darkness. He bent his head forward to cover the silver cloud with his arms of safety. Just as he inhaled the beauty of the mist, the darkness emerged and pounced on the silver cloud leaving nothing but a damp sparkle on Theo's chest where blood spurted from an open wound over his heart. He lay bleeding on the ground while the consuming darkness crawled away.

Theo woke from his nightmare, drenched in sweat and tears. They weren't tears of losing a battle. They were tears of something being pulled from his heart. He wiped the sweat from his hands and his chest with the wool blanket and curled into a little ball where he could weep for a loss that had exhausted every muscle of his body. At first he refused to believe the tears were any more than a bad dream, but his mind succumbed to knowing he had seen another precognition of something to come.

A loud blast from a horn outside the tent zone woke and warned the boys to be ready by 0500 hours. Frowsy-headed kids rolled over, ignoring the blast, but six older boys and one blind rat thirteen-year-old jumped from their cots and made short order of washroom and dress time. A new day with new adventure promised Theo the nightmare would be left behind.

Theo was dressed and ready for a day of instruction and challenge in the wilderness. After all, isn't that what camp stories were made of? Out of habit, Theo reached under the cot for the canvas bag to hang from his belt and hold the necessities the camp leaders suggested for the day in the wilderness: one knife, one fifty-foot-piece of cording, a piece of flint, and a whistle.

Theo remembered how his integrated robotic intelligence system was programmed to remind him to put a nutrition bar in his backpack each day. *Well, sorry, IRIS. I don't have my backpack, and I don't have a nutrition bar. Thanks for the mental reminder, anyway.* He grinned in the dark and continued weaving his bag onto his belt. *I do wish I had a flashlight, though.* He never needed one before because Murphy's collar always lit his way. *I need to get Murphy back from Kuhn. If I had Murphy, I could... No! Stop it now!* Theo grunted aloud as his thoughts argued with his heart. *Face it. I don't have him. Maybe it's best. Gracie and I survived the wilderness without him. I know I can do this. I just needed a reason to step up and prove to...prove to...to...to everyone...to myself. I can do this!*

As if thoughts moved through the airwaves, a black snout poked out of the covers that Theo had half-heartedly tossed in a "make the bed" fashion. Though the snout did not catch Theo's attention, the sound of a wet sneeze made him jerk up on his haunches from where he pulled his gear from under the bed.

"Murph!" Theo lunged over the cot where a beagle's head had worked its way up to the pillow. "How long have you been in here? Man, it's good to see you, ol' boy." He tousled the dog's floppy ears

RENDERED

with one hand and pushed his face into the dog's neck just as Murphy grinned in a pant and rolled to his back for a belly rub.

"How'd you get in here? How'd you get away? Aw, Murph, you can't stay in here. You've got a mission to do, and I've got a…" The sound of the tent flap popping open made Theo jump to his feet and throw the wool blanket up over the pillow.

A grunting exhale pushed from Theo's lungs as he flipped his gear bag onto his belt and turned, nearly putting him nose to nose with his survival leader. Dan tipped his head back to look out of the bottom of his eyes as if to show himself a larger person than Theo; though, Theo's growth had given him the height of a tall man.

"You excited about something, Friedrich?" Dan kept his voice at a low growl, not to prevent waking the sleeping boys in the tent, but to make Theo lean in to listen.

"What? Uh, no. No, sir. Just caught a good bit of morning air in my lungs. I mean, yes, sir. I'm ready for today's survival instruction, sir." Theo stumbled off guard.

Leader Dan sniffed and pivoted before he bent to walk back out of the tent without any of the sleeping boys knowing he was there.

Whew! Don't know if I'm off to a good start or not. Theo rummaged through a pile at the foot of his cot. Might need this, and this, who knows, maybe this. He picked up a fork from the dining hall, fishing line wadded in a knot, a thick piece of glass from the bottom of a broken bottle, two matches he had found beside last night's campfire, and his toothbrush and stuffed them into his pack.

"Later, Murphy." A quick pat didn't disturb the dog, recharging in his sleep.

By 0600 hours, seven boys were squatting at the edge of the woods, looking up at Leader Dan, ready to learn and obey instructions. Dan stood with his hands on his hips and looked down at the boys, relishing the feeling of power he felt by towering over the boys, especially the ones who would surely pass him in height in the months to follow. He wanted the boys to be putty in his hands, and he knew the best way to mold them was to win them over with flattery.

"Looks like I've got a winning crew this year, stronger and more intelligent young men than what I've had in survival training in the past. Looks like I've drawn the aces of the deck today. It'll be my pleasure to work with you, boys." Dan allowed a pause, letting his words paint overconfident smirks on the faces of the campers.

To hide a nervousness of knowing the boys would have less training than they needed, Dan shifted his arms to cross against his muscular chest before he continued. "Lessons will be shorter this morning. I'll talk about surroundings as we hike up the road where we'll begin a wilderness survival trek. Your job is to return to camp before midnight, in one piece."

A slight snicker passed among the boys as they hoped for an easy task; though, they felt as if bolts of lightning had passed through their hearts. A few older boys blocked coughs with their fists to cover physical signs of uneasiness. Only Günter straightened his back and sat taller in a physical show of accepting a challenge. Theo noticed his silent enemy's reaction to Leader Dan's words.

"Boys"—Dan forcefully punctuated his first word to belittle the campers—"the challenge will require some thinking. Since some of you aren't used to thinking without your mommas around, I'll put you into groups of two." He stopped and lifted the corner of his mouth as a couple sharp chuckles came from the campers. "Now, if you've already done this advanced math, you'll see that we don't divide evenly." Again he paused as the boys glanced around their group. "One of you will have to go on his own." He raised a palm to the group that emitted a slight chatter.

"Hans and Ira," Dan pointed at the youngest and a sixteen-year-old. "You're a pair. Harvey and Nicolaus, pair up." Two more boys nodded first to Leader Dan, then to each other. "That leaves Rambert, Theo, and Günter." Dan gestured toward the group.

Impulsively, Theo jumped to his feet. "I'll go alone, sir."

"Hey, no one asked you to be a martyr." Günter slowly stood and lifted his shoulders and stepped to go chest to chest with Theo.

"I'll…" Neither boy reacted to the sound that came as Dan started to speak then dropped his arms to his side and squinted out of one eye to see how the two young men would settle.

"Sorry, Günter," Theo grinned at the grimace on Günter's face. "That's kind of you to worry about me, but I stood first, so I'll go it alone." He gestured toward the third boy who was beginning to stand from his squat. "This time you can show Rambert all you know about survival. You two can learn together."

Before Günter could react to the insult, Theo turned and stepped close to Leader Dan. "I'll go alone." Theo repeated the offer to seal the decision while squatting boys stole glances from Günter to the ground, knowing Theo had thrown down the gauntlet of challenge.

During the three-hour hike that finished out the morning, Leader Dan checked his compass often and wrote his bearings on a scrap of paper tucked beside the pencil in his pocket. He knew the area, and he knew the challenge would only be successful if he crossed a few rivers and doubled back several times to confuse the campers, even those who were familiar with the territory. Using more valleys than hills to wander through the deep woods, he did his best to keep the boys from having visuals to mark their trails. His own experience as a tracker would be a necessity to return to camp unscathed. He patted the scrap with notes tucked in his chest pocket and looked at the sun perched directly overhead, casting no shadows one way or another.

With a fisted arm held in the air, Leader Dan stopped the hike and turned to face the approaching boys. Teenage arms began to stiffen into a tracking dog's point as boys huddled into a mass that faced their leader. Günter was first to bark out a command.

"Halt!"

"Heil Hitler!" Seven voices pumped out the call. One voice added a lighthearted huff for remembering to respond just like the German campers.

"All right, boys. You can throw down your rucksacks and eat a bite before you begin your trek back to camp."

Plopping noises responded to Leader Dan's suggestion. One boy reached a squat before he noticed that the others still stood at attention, waiting for their leader's further instruction. His mouth hung open as he looked wide-eyed around at the other boys and rose up to join the stiff stance of obedience.

Dan sucked in the dusky forest air. He loved the scent of the outdoors. Unlike Fritz Kuhn, he had no wish to train boys by showing how weak they were. Raised in the Midwest, Dan was born with an insatiable desire to inhale the outdoors and let it thrill and fill every vein that pumped through his soul. He couldn't explain it.

At age sixteen, Dan watched his uncle's family structure collapse when the stock market crashed and crumbled the foundations of home, job, and economy. From his Midwest home, the young Dan felt reverberations when his uncle fought and surrendered to the personal battle of keeping a family fed in the New Jersey world of job loss and forced poverty. He only knew his cousins by name, but he still ran behind the barn and threw up at the news that his cousins buried their father and wondered which sin was worse—taking his own life or the government taking every penny he had earned.

By the early 1930s, Dan's family had struggles of their own when their land, livestock, and source of income were buried under the dirt of the Dust Bowl. Dan admired his parents' internal fortitude that fought to survive.

At age nineteen, Dan answered a newspaper add to move to New Jersey and join the Civilian Conservation Corps, a program initiated by President Roosevelt. Nine camps of men between the ages of seventeen and twenty-five were hired to work in state forests and parks. Dan knew this job was a gift from God to help the financial burden at home and to fulfill his love for being outdoors.

Dan grew in wisdom about man and nature. He was at home in the forests, and no trail had a challenge he wouldn't face. Thus, in 1932, he was hired by Colonel H. Norman Schwarzkopf, superintendent of the New Jersey State Police, to help search the countryside for a wealthy aviator's young son. The search took him to rough woodlands and city parks before the kidnapped, twenty-month-old son of Charles Lindbergh was found in the woods where he had been killed by a blow that fractured his skull. The sight of coming across the knoll and seeing Schwarzkopf with the tiny child draped across his arms stirred an unrest in his soul. By 1935 when a German immigrant was executed for the death of the Lindbergh baby, the mental picture of Schwarzkopf and the baby resurfaced and again agitated his soul.

In the summer of the following year, Dan took a job teaching outdoor skills at a camp for children of German immigrants in an effort to forgive and to believe a country of people could not be judged by a führer or by a madman immigrant. He held to his Midwestern belief in the good of mankind, and he vowed to use the bund camp to counter hatred from the inside.

Leader Dan glanced at the eager faces. "Congratulations on a great hike. From here you'll follow clues to numbered checkpoints. Each checkpoint will present a challenge. When you complete the challenge, find direction to the next checkpoint. Some of you will take the challenge. Some of you will decline and lose points." Dan scanned the group, allowing a slight nod at Theo and again at Günter. "Some will be challenged just to hike the course and return to camp." He paused to allow a few nervous snickers. "Finish the challenge course or not, return to camp by midnight. Campers completing the most challenges will be rewarded."

Leader Dan paused in his list of instructions as he handed each group and Theo a paper with a list of challenges. He paused and crossed his arms against his chest as the boys looked at their paper of notes.

Theo mentally checked through his list.
Camp Coordinates: 41.0292° N, 74.7235° W

1. Chop one-inch diameter log using your gear. Stow half log in pack.
2. Carve spindle to use later for a bow-and-drill fire. Pack.
3. Apply one arm sling in group for duration.
4. Make primitive trap and strap to rucksack.
5. Use shell casing to make arrow.
6. Use signal mirror at meadow flat rock until fire tower waves white flag.

7. Dress injury noted on tree north of fire tower. Build stretcher and transport injured.
8. Find, draw, and name edible or medicinal plant. Pack a stalk.
9. Tie Prusik knot around vine or stem. Pack.
10. Make a Swiss seat. Wear to camp.

"Any questions or instruction need repeated?" Grins and shuffles assured the camp leader that the boys were ready to begin the challenge.

"Good." Dan held up one finger to bring attention back to his face. "Any groups of two that join forces will be disqualified. If you think you need to play together to get back to camp, I'll be sure you entertain the rest of camp tonight with fist boxing until only one of you is left standing. You work in the pairs I've appointed. No other." He sucked in a breath and looked at the boys already weary from the hike. "If you're smart, you'll eat." Dan unhooked a bag dangling from his pack and tossed it to the youngest who didn't disappoint him in leaving his sack of sandwich and apples on the table in the camp mess hall.

"See you tonight, boys. If you're lucky." Dan raised one eyebrow and spun to walk away from the seven youths left standing in the woods.

Boys scrambled to dig food from their packs. Theo drank from his canteen before eating his sandwich. He knew he would get more mileage from the food if he tricked his stomach into feeling full before beginning the sandwich. Two bites into his sandwich, he scanned the area and tipped his head back hoping to pick up the scent of a forest stream.

"C'mon, Rambert," Günter barked at his teammate. "We'll start walking."

"But, Günter, shouldn't we let our leg muscles get a rest before we begin again?" Rambert held his sandwich between his knee and his mouth as he half lay propped against a fallen tree.

"We'll rest when we need to, Rambert. Now let's go." Günter looked at his teammate, controlling the urge to notice the expressions on faces around him until he intentionally looked Theo in the eye. "I don't plan to be the last one back." He turned again to face Rambert as he pushed his apple and sandwich into the canvas bag hanging at his side and started walking into the cover of woods.

Rambert swallowed and gave Theo a quick glance before he scrambled to his feet and carried a half-eaten sandwich and apple as he jogged into the woods where Günter disappeared.

The last team of boys left the site where Leader Dan had ended their morning hike. Theo looked up through the canopy of treetops from where his head rested against a log on the forest floor. He intentionally gave himself time to rest after the hike, letting his body absorb the light lunch. He looked at a frog sitting on a leaf tucked under the log.

"I hope I haven't screwed up by waiting so long to begin. Whaddaya think, Mr. Frog? Time for me to do some jumpin'?" He looked back up at the sky that shot rays of light through breaks in the branches. "Had to wait until I could tell which direction was west. Sure didn't want to spend half an hour walking the wrong way while the straight-up sun refused to gimme a shadow of direction!" He nudged the frog that snuggled under the log.

Theo picked a thin branch from the forest floor. "Ya know, this looks about like the one-inch log I'm needing for the challenge." He propped one end on a nearby rock and stepped on the branch until it snapped. "Yep. One piece for you oh, Leader Danno, and one for Ol' Sol to tell me which way to go." In a clearing, he batoned one piece of the branch into the ground before he put the other piece in his pack.

He returned to the fallen log. "Okay, Mr. Frog. You're not a real big guy, so I'm going to assume you're not too far from water. Care to tell me where I can refill my canteen?" Theo squinted past the trees surrounding him and begged his ears to hear a stream. Walking away from the lunch spot, Theo stuck sticks upright in the ground as he walked away from the path where Dan had led them into the forest.

"Nice." Theo noticed a sparkle from sunshine against a rock ahead. "Must be a wet rock." Within minutes, Theo dipped his canteen into a stream before he secured it with a rope around his belt and followed the trail of upright sticks back to the lunch spot.

"Well, all right then." Theo grinned at the upright stick he had pounded into the clearing and noted the shadow cast from the moving sun. "So now I know which direction will head me back into camp." Using the direction of the shadow as a compass to begin his hike, he silently prayed the path back would be as simple to understand. Although the sun did not disappoint him in showing him direction, it joined forces with the thick forest that betrayed him and refused to let rays pass through the thick matting of undergrowth.

By midafternoon Theo had given up on following the course of the sun under the dark canopy above his head. "What's going on up there? Why's it so dark?" He cocked his head to hear a pattering sound. "Wow. This is really a dense wood. I think it's raining, but down here I'm not getting wet. I'm pretty sure I'm hearing rain."

He felt the wrist computer in his pocket. "Hey, IRIS, how about you put a man on my nop and drop a pin. Or better yet, IRIS, how about you just talk to me and tell me where to go!" Tired from walking and anxious from not knowing where he was, Theo spoke to the nothingness of the forest in a quavering voice, not caring that no one could hear him. "Just you wait. When I get back with Murphy, we'll figure out this blasted forest."

"Murphy!" Impulsively, Theo yelled into the thick forest that swallowed his voice.

A space of light contrasted with the dark in the trees ahead. "Maybe a clearing up there..." Theo chugged down the last of the water in his canteen and took off in a full run toward the opening. The forest rain had forced runnels under the matted ground. Theo was caught off guard when his foot slipped on the wet leaf-covered mud that ended at a rock wall where the river lay fifteen feet below. The momentum of his run hitting the slick mud gave no mercy as his body fell over the cliff.

Theo bounced off protruding rocks and even a tree that grew from the side of the rocky ledge before his body hit and wrapped around a boulder.

Beaten

A RACCOON'S NOSE NUDGED THE hair hanging down on the sand. The smell of the unconscious body on the rock teased the animal's senses but offered nothing to the creature that waddled to the river.

By the time the body groaned, there was neither moonlight nor day's sunshine. The sky peered down through a crease of daybreak that hung over the young man beginning to waken and writhe. A soft grunt followed as Theo's hand wiggled between his face and the rocky ground.

He fingered the side of his head. "Dirt? Aw, crap. Dried blood." He pressed his body off the boulder. "Ugh. Head pound." He leaned against the cliff where he had fallen the night before. "Welp, found water. Thanks for nothing, IRIS."

The sun stood at full attention of midday before Theo opened his eyes again. "Water. Sure. Drag over for drink. Water for breakfast." He rubbed his empty stomach.

Theo plopped on the bank and cupped water into his mouth before he looked around. A wet hand rubbed through his hair, followed by a rock tossed into the river. "Well, Günter, I'm throwing in the towel. Looks like you've beaten me. You win!" he yelled into sounds of water tumbling against rocks in the stream. "Okay! I'm giving up! Anyone out there who can tell me how to get back to camp?" Realizing his yelling was only making his headache worse, Theo dropped his voice. "Pretty sure I'm late getting back anyway."

"Let's see. I gotta get out of this ravine. Where though? Better try the compass." Theo unhooked the carabiner that clipped the compass to his rucksack and awkwardly turned it. "Red in the shed. Zikes, what the heck am I doing? Orienteering on computer was easier. Guess I thought with my nop I'd never need a compass." He huffed a quick laugh. "Who knew?"

Turning upstream, the lost camper kept an eye on the cliff looking for footholds and a way back up to the forest. The steep climb agitated nerves around his old leg injury and pulsed a trickle of blood from his forehead.

A startled blue jay hopped onto a fallen tree as a pack came flying over the ridge and hung on a brush pile. Theo slung a leg over the edge. "I'm up!" He rolled his head to one side and saw the small black eyes staring back in curiosity. "Hey, little fella."

The blue jay fluttered his wings and took one last glare before flying away.

"Okay, fine chicken little! I was probably just going to eat ya anyway!" Theo sat up chuckling at his own joke. "I shouldn't have said that. Now I'm really hungry. Nothin' but ground cover. Where are the wild berries they always find in storybooks?" He picked a small daisylike flower from the ground. "Humph." The fragrant flower spun in his fingers. "Wait a minute. I think you were in one of our lessons the other day. Maybe." Theo crushed the chamomile flower and leaves before strapping them to his head with a bandana. "Don't know if this will stop the bleeding but got number 8 checked off the list." He dropped another flower into his pack.

By late morning Theo's stomach and head contended for top pain maker. "I'm starving. Where's that little blue jay now? I'd even settle for a mouse…" He caught sight of a colorful bug dragging along the bark of a tree. "Ugh. I'd even eat you, but your pretty little body tells me that I'd be very, very sick if I ate you." He reached up and flicked the bug off the tree and watched its body spiral down to the forest overgrowth. "So long, sucker!"

Theo leaned on his outstretched arm letting his hand feel the rough bark. "I'd even eat a tree if…Wait a minute! Get your brain out of your stomach and think, Theo!" He studied the trees. "Hello, where are you, Mr. Maple?" He raised his eyebrows as fond memories came back from a time when he and his parents had traveled to Vermont for an old-time adventure in tapping for maple syrup.

RENDERED

Slowly walking around the forest, Theo studied the leaves until he saw a small grouping of maples. He slapped his hand against one of the big trees. "Well, you big guys are off the hook this time. I wanna sapling." He wrapped his fingers around a small trunk. "Hello, youngster. What are you? A teenager?"

Theo pulled a knife from the sheath on his belt and mercilessly stabbed at the bark. Some curling bark gave way, but other bark held fast against the whaling blade. Too hungry to think, Theo recklessly pounded against the tree until a snap signaled a victim in the war between bark and blade. The knife blade fell to the ground, leaving the handle tucked inside Theo's fist.

"Augh!" Theo fell to his knees and raked through the thick grasses at the base of the tree until he felt the stab of the disabled blade. He tried to plunge the thin blade into the bark, but the slick metal was impossible to grip. He tipped his head back and again screamed.

Over the past year he had acted recklessly, but between Murphy's robotics and Gracie's common sense, he hadn't done much independent thinking. Lost in the New Jersey woods, he stood alone in unfamiliar territory. Theo exhaled and looked at the blade. "Okay, God, you made this tree. Can you help me take it apart?" With deliberate moves, he scraped the soft exposed wood until he could lodge the blade. He slid the handle onto the blade and drilled it into the tree.

Satisfied by the sweet sap that sprang from the hole, Theo slung his rucksack across his shoulder. He followed a stream that gave no hint of altitude but promised a refreshing drink and a path through the forest.

The tilt of the sun proved it had been at least twenty-four hours since Leader Dan tossed a sack of lunch at the boys. Empty swallows taunted Theo's hungry stomach. The stream beside him held a hope of food. Nights in Germany's forests had taught him two things. One, he'd want fire for warmth through the night, and two, a matted trail in the grass would bring food to him if he failed to catch a fish. Pulling the fishing line from his pack, the weary traveler half-heartedly welcomed the challenge to get offerings of nature.

Three long, skinny tree limbs held strands of filament dangling in the stream while the other ends sat wedged in the bank. Crawdads hung tied to the ends of the fishing line that danced in the current along the shore. Theo smiled at the thought of the feast he hoped to catch from the limb lines and glanced up at the late afternoon sky.

"Hold on, Ol' Sol. I'd rather use you than a bow drill to start a fire." He carefully pulled the broken bottle from his pack. He didn't notice when the two matches he had stashed fell onto the ground.

Theo piled twigs and leaves for tinder. The sun agreed to shine a ray through the thick end of the broken glass until a wisp of smoke gave birth to a flame in the magnified tinder pile. He leaned down and softly blew the little flame, feeding it with twigs until the rocks held a blazing fire. With firelight and waning daylight, Theo pulled brush and fallen limbs into an arch close to the fire. "Not exactly a bow drill, but it's a fire. Sorry, Leader Danno." Theo grinned at the nickname.

"Shelter." Theo glanced down at the river where one of his limb lines shook from the movement of a fish. "And dinner!" He let out a whoop as he hobbled to the river. "Gracie, look at me now!"

"Ah, sweet Gracie, you're in my thoughts even now. At least you have easier days in your boarding school." Something was comforting in watching the clouds scoot past in the late summer sky.

Never would Theo realize that the young *Fräulein*, had earlier been in the same forest as she searched for her American friend.

Morning welcomed the overnight traveler with two more fish caught on his lines. "Breakfast of champion fishermen…and raccoons…" Theo tossed fish scraps to a raccoon squatting beside the river. "Help yourself and you're welcome my—"

A shrill sound interrupted both voice and babbling river. Theo scanned the valley. *What kinda animal…* He held his breath to listen for another sound. *Where?* The raccoon rose on his haunches and pointed his nose upstream. No sound came.

"Whoop." Pause. A little more air pushed through Theo's voice. "Whoop." He squinted to see up the hill. *Curiosity killed the cat, but I can't stand not knowing.* "Whoop," a little louder.

RENDERED

Theo slapped at his shorts to knock off dirt that clung to the coarse fabric. "Nothing." He swiveled. The upper forest seemed less friendly as matted brush formed walls.

Again, a sharp cry came through the forest. Theo jerked an ear toward the scream that faded into scratchy whimpers. *What? Who?* He pulled himself through the tight undergrowth and caught himself in a fall as his legs slid into nothingness. "Augh!" This time it was his own voice that screamed.

His arms held his weight and threatened to pull out of their sockets. Theo pushed his head back to look up at his hands still holding to the matted undergrowth. He felt for footholds in the hole. Running in place, he dug the toes of his boots into the crumbling dirt.

Where's ground? God, please help me! Theo stopped flailing long enough to realize his feet were swinging in an undercut bluff. *Gotta pull—*

Through pull-ups and grasping brush that grew out of the bluff, Theo balanced his waist on the ledge and again swung his legs back up. The surge of adrenaline and the threat of the fall left him shaking and sore. Cautiously, he rolled onto his stomach and saw a thirty-foot drop off the side of the bluff. *What just happened? Really? Throw myself over a cliff again?*

He lay sweating, not wanting to move. Again he heard the scream, more like a wail. Theo raised his head. *Down there.* His eyes scanned for movement, something wounded.

Not my problem. Not my prob... The young man wrestled between reason and responsibility. *I just need to get outa here. Probably just a hurt animal. Nothing I can do to help. Not safe...*

Wails interrupted his thoughts. *Human? No, no, no, no...I can't, can't get down there.*

He rocked back and forth as he stood up. *Can't get down...need something...* Mechanically, his mind searched for a path down into the ravine. His eyes jerked as he pushed himself from tree to tree. His hand grasped something. A rope. No, vine.

"Okay. This'll do." He yanked so hard the momentum tipped him backward as the loose vine swung through the air. "Augh! If I don't get my head on straight, I'll kill myself." He tossed the vine to the ground.

Again the wail.

"Just stop!" Theo screamed with all his breath.

The wail came again, almost in the form of a word.

Theo tipped his head to listen.

"Noooo. Help."

Theo balled up his fists and shook them at empty skies. "How can I help?" He studied the edge of the bluff and the ground at his feet. "Vine…more vine…rope…"

With new energy he searched and pulled at the undergrowth until he found a vine that snaked from one tree to the next. He pulled at vines, hoping one grew into the bark of a tree.

The wail weakened as Theo searched through vines on the forest floor for a makeshift rappelling rope. Fearful of losing his footing again, he wrapped the end of a vine around a small tree and attached the middle of his camp rope with a Prusik knot. The other ends of the rope wrapped around his waist.

"Where are you?"

A scratchy sound came back to him.

"Louder! I can't see you. Where are you?" His voice bordered on anger from not knowing what to do. He turned an ear toward a boulder farther down.

"Louder! Louder! I'm not coming if I can't—"

In an effort that took full breath, the voice interrupted, "Help!"

That was it! Theo heard the voice from behind the boulder down the cliff. He held the vine and scooted down the rocky soil, half squatting, half sitting, and sliding until he passed enough of the boulder to see a human leg dressed in canvas shorts.

"I'm here. I'm here. I'm…Günter!"

Günter's head rolled, but his eyelids closed on a tear-streaked face.

"No! No, no, no, no. Günter! Look at me! Open your eyes! Open!" Theo grabbed the collar below the closed eyes. "Open! Stay with me!" Theo heard his own voice waver between threat and panic.

He released the collar and ran his hand down to where the bolder lay over Günter's foot.

"Okay. Günter, listen to me. Breathe, Günter. Open your eyes. Fight with me, Günter. Come on! Fight!"

Theo braced himself against the boulder but knew it was wedged from a roll down the hill. "Günter, talk to me!" Theo yelled at the boy who had been his enemy, but he knew to look at Günter's swollen face would weaken him.

Too heavy. Move. Wedged. Heavy. That's it. Wedge.

Rocks of all sizes lay in the field beneath the bluff. Theo searched and worked a plan. *Rock. Under opera house. Heavy. Wedge.*

Scrambled thoughts formed a plan. He remembered when Gracie had moved a cement cap on a tunnel under the German opera house. The petite teen was too weak to lift the cement disk, but by wedging her boot and expanding the hole, she escaped the tunnel.

"Always with me, Gracie. Always with me." Theo hoped to wedge the boulder and dig under until he could free Günter's leg.

For the better part of an hour Theo wedged and dug using flat rocks and talked to a young man who faded in and out of consciousness. He dug under Günter's leg, creating a channel under the crushed foot.

Screams of pain and screams of determination filled the rock valley as Theo locked his arms under Günter's shoulders and pulled the body from under the boulder. He collapsed on the ground, realizing the air stung his hands, rubbed raw from digging.

Theo ripped at his shirt. "Not exactly a sling, sorry, Danno, but I'm wrapping my hands instead."

Crafting a body sling to drag Günter seemed to take hours. "Not really pretty my friend," Theo stood the branches on end to show a boy who was senseless from pain. "For now, it's gotta do." He dropped the frame to the ground and rolled Günter enough to center him on the stretcher. Again, Günter wailed as his weight shifted when Theo lifted the branches and started to drag the deadweight across the meadow.

"Sorry, man. Gotta follow the river. S'only way out."

Trudging in silence, Theo pulled the bunglesome stretcher until a branch of the frame snapped. Cries from pain and cries from exhaustion were buried in the babbling river.

Interrogation

"Have a seat, Miss Foster." The headmaster stood then sat again in nervous agitation, afraid the people in the room would sense that he was on the verge of losing control.

"We have been told, Miss Foster, that you can help us find the missing girl, Gracie Cooper." Every eye in the room focused on Nancy Foster, distracted only by the headmaster's shoe scuffing under the chair where he sat. "It has been reported that you may know where she is."

Expressionless, the young teacher looked directly at the headmaster, not in defiance but in determination. "I thank you for your attention, Headmaster, but I don't know why you credit me with having information as to her location. It seems to me that as she left during school hours, it would be difficult for me to be both in and out of my classroom at the same time and know where every girl on this campus spends each moment of the day."

The headmaster glanced up from where he rummaged through a folder of paper as if hoping a clue would drop off one of the pages. "No need to get sharp with me, Miss Foster. It's my understanding—and the understanding of several of us at this table"—he gesticulated with a flip of his hand—"that you have had a conversation with this girl concerning a map."

"I teach history and geography, Headmaster. It's not unusual to discuss my subject matter with my students. Perhaps you could better spend your time questioning teachers who fall short on classroom instruction. I can hardly be criticized for doing my job. Your albatross is not my matter, sir. I'm maintaining my own boat on this ocean of education. I didn't bring on this tempest."

"You're changing the subject, Foster!" The headmaster's voice rose briefly before he inhaled deeply and mentally reminded himself that he needed information that would only come if Nancy Foster felt he was on her side. "Uh, hum." He lifted a glass of water to clear his throat but did not drink before resetting the glass for fear the nervous shaking of his hands would be detected.

"Please, Miss Foster, we need your compliance. The state doesn't take lightly to us losing the charges in our care. It's hard enough to garner state funds to educate girls. We certainly need to be ready to defend our school when the press gets word that we've lost a guppy in this ocean of education." A short-lived swell of laughter gave all around the table a chance to break from the tension in the room.

"Gracie Cooper is not a guppy, sir." Nancy Foster stood her ground. "She may be new to Blair Academy, but she's intelligent and educated. She's advanced in many areas. I've even wondered if my lectures are too simple for her. I've had no private conversations with the young lady, though you accuse me differently, Headmaster, but I've seen dreams lying deep in her eyes. I do know she has friends. Friends you would covet to have in your personal address book," Miss Foster paused with a raised eyebrow in the direction of the head of the table. "No, no, Headmaster. She's not a guppy. Gracie is a starfish."

Refusing to be bested by the calm of the young teacher, the headmaster slammed shut the folder and glared at Nancy Foster. "I don't care if she's a starfish, guppy, or whale! You must not cover for this girl and try to save her from her disobedience to this institution! You are known for taking the sides of errant girls on this campus. You can't save them all!"

"I'm not trying to save them all." The teacher looked down at her lap where she noticed she was wringing her hands as she brought her voice under control. "Right now, I'm just trying to save one."

The headmaster leaned forward in his chair with his clasped hands on the table. "We have interrogated girls from your classroom, Miss Foster. It seems there was an incident during a lecture several days ago that involved a map." He sat back to demonstrate his control. "Now, Miss Foster, the secretary is ready to record all you say.

Perhaps you can tell about this incident and keep regard for the fact that your words will be recorded. Truth is of the utmost importance."

"Truth? The truth, Headmaster, is that I reprimanded Gracie for drawing during one of my lectures. Upon confrontation, I discovered she was drawing a map of the area of the United States straight from my description. It was remarkably well done. I complimented her on her work."

"Was there anything noteworthy on this map drawing?" A dean of the academy took his turn at questioning, more out of curiosity than of prying.

"Detail was just as I had lectured." She smiled at the dean, appreciative of his kind expression. "There was one location on the map that had not been in the lecture. So, I questioned, and she explained it was the location where she last saw her friends…" She paused briefly to turn and look at the headmaster before finishing. "Mrs. Roosevelt and Ms. Earhart."

"What child doesn't have fancy dreams?" A voice piped up at the table.

"No, it's probable truth." All turned to look at the registrar of the academy who also sat with a file of papers in front of her. "According to her admission records, she was brought by a Miss…" She fumbled through the stack. "Ah, here it is. Miss Hickok, personal secretary to Mrs. Roosevelt. We have no other paperwork suggesting her roots or why Mrs. Roosevelt would pay to enroll an urchin in Blair Academy, but it seems good proof that the White House holds Blair Academy in high standing."

"And will dangle us over the pit of hell itself if we have to report the child has disappeared from our campus!" The headmaster spoke to all, especially to his own fears.

"Please, Miss Foster, think back. Was there anything else noted on the map that could give us a clue as to her whereabouts?" Again the dean spoke up.

"No. I'm sorry." Nancy Foster shook her head and looked around the table, unafraid to let her eyes rest on the headmaster. "There's something special about this girl. Believe me, I have wrestled with knowing she's gone and trying to think if at any time she said or did anything that I could use as a clue. I can think of nothing to help. Her absence wrings my soul. We speak as if she were running from us. In my heart, I wonder if she was not running away but rather running to someplace or someone." Again she shook her head and let her eyes close. "I understand your concern for this institution, and I share that concern. I just pray nothing bad happens to her."

Nancy Foster stood and dismissed herself without any further words. The click of her Mary Jane heels echoed against the wooden floor. Even the sound of the secretary setting her pen down on the table seemed amplified in the silent room.

The young teacher walked slowly across the campus, clutching the collar of her cardigan, not to keep out the evening breeze but to hold in the heart that seemed swollen and ready to bleed. Nancy looked up at the darkening sky, clear with a cool touch and filled with a galaxy of stars.

Tell me, stars, where is she? She's out there, somewhere. Please watch over that sweet child. Who is she? Where has she come from? I don't know. But I feel in my soul that she needs me. Nancy eased down onto a bench and watched the stars reflect in the campus pond. The tower clock chimed across the water.

"Nine o'clock already." Nancy stood and pulled the comb that held her hair in a sophisticated knot on the back of her head. *Better stop for a cup of tea at my apartment before we converge on poor Klara. I may need to stay after the interrogation committee leaves her room.*

In a moment's gesture, Nancy flung her hand from mouth to stars and blew a kiss across the sky.

"Klara! Stop your incessant crying and tell us what you know. Where is Gracie?" The headmaster's voice ricocheted off the dorm room wall where the metal bed sat empty and lifeless against the open windowsill. "Somebody shut that blasted window. I don't need the wind blowing in my face to taunt me. Her disobedience should not punish us!" Headmaster Breed was known for his calm, and his terse speech was evidence that he was shaken by Gracie's disappearance.

Miss Foster's arm felt secure around Klara's shoulders, but nothing could soothe the young girl's heart sinking deeper into her chest. "Klara, please, you need to help us. We don't want to punish or hurt Gracie. Tell us what you know so we can help her."

"Klara, you risk being sent back to the orphanage if you are harboring information that we need to know." The headmaster searched for compassion in his heart, but pressure robbed the softness from his voice, knowing the incident would throw Blair Academy under scrutiny of the benefactors. He worried what the commissioner would do when word got back to the administration that a student boarder not only ran away but escaped out a window in broad daylight. He wrung his hands and paced from head to foot of the silent bed wedged against the window.

"Dr. Breed, may I have some time with Klara?"

The headmaster gave one nod to Miss Foster as he reached a hand to Klara's shoulder with a single pat. "Yes, it's getting late, Nan. Calm the child and perhaps she'll tell what she knows. We'll meet in the faculty council room before classes tomorrow morning. Good night, Miss Foster. Klara." The worry did not leave the headmaster's brow as he left the dormitory room.

"Klara…"

"I'm sorry, Miss Foster. I, I want to, to help, really. I, I just don't…" Klara dropped her head, sobbing again. "I don't know. I don't know anything."

Nancy Foster knew Klara was truthful and was hurting from the loss of her friend. "I'll leave. You rest. Perhaps tomorrow something will be clearer to us." Her fingers pulled hair away from Klara's damp eyes. "She'll be all right, Klara. I'm sure she's found a home for the night." The young teacher walked to the door and turned before pulling the door closed behind her.

"My apartment is at the end of the first-floor hall. Please come to me if you remember anything."

Though she squeezed her eyes closed, Klara heard the door click shut. Heartbroken, she went to the empty bed and lay back with her head on Gracie's pillow. Klara watched wispy clouds bouncing off moonbeams.

"Gracie, where are you? Clouds, please take me to her," Klara whispered into the night sky.

Klara rubbed the back of her neck as she rolled from Gracie's pillow. "What?" She blinked against the light breeze coming through the open window. "Morning? Ugh. No. It's still the middle of the night." She lay with an arm draped across her forehead. "This has to be the worst pillow…" Klara rolled to her side and punched up at the pillow that had for weeks cradled Gracie's head. "Ow! Whoever heard of a hard pillow!" Again, Klara punched at the pillow and realized her fist hit against something inside the pillow cover. "What in the world?"

Klara pulled a book from inside the cover. "Really, Gracie? You slept with a book in your pillow? *Dark Victory*." Klara sat up and let her feet fall to the floor. "I never saw you reading this book. It doesn't even look like a book that you'd like." She looked around the room. Someone had found Gracie's satchel and set it on the desk the two girls shared. Klara carried the book to Gracie's satchel to slip inside. Lifting the flap, Klara saw the map Gracie had drawn.

"Uhh." Klara sucked in a gulp of night air as she pulled the folded paper from Gracie's bag. "Oh, Gracie! I do know where you are! I don't know where you're headed, but I know how you're getting there! Oh! Miss Foster! I must tell…" Not caring that her hair and clothes were tousled from a restless sleep, Klara ran from the room with the folded map in her hand.

Night Search

KLARA WAS SURE SHE HADN'T slept in the sedan that pulled to the side of the road, but her deep breathing told a different story.

Hours earlier after finding Gracie's map, Klara had carried her shoes and tiptoe-ran down to the end of the first-floor hall where Nancy Foster's home was nestled in a large dormitory room. Klara's soft knocking was scarcely loud enough to disturb anyone, but after only a few knocks, the door was opened by a young teacher afflicted by a restless night.

"Klara. Come in." Nancy pulled the teen who hugged shoes and a piece of paper to her chest. Although the boarding school was silent, the young teacher glanced up the hall to see if anyone else had heard the midnight visitor's rap on the door. All lay so silently that Nancy was sure her heartbeat was echoing off the dormitory walls.

"Here," With a quick whisper, Klara extended her fisted hand.

The perplexed woman knitted her brow. "Shoes?"

"Oh! Oh, no! Not shoes! I mean, they are my shoes, but I didn't mean to give you my shoes. That's the wrong hand. I mean, I didn't...I should have..." Klara stumbled over her words in her hurry to show what she had found. "I found this!" She thrust out her other hand.

Klara's confusion seemed fitting for the hour of the night, but Nancy Foster suspected this was a necessary disruption. She unfolded the paper. "A map. Gracie's map from my lecture." She looked up at Klara's wide eyes. "Is there something I'm missing here?"

"It's Gracie! Where she is!"

Miss Foster's heart leaped, but she was too familiar with excitable teen girls to get drawn in too quickly. "Klara, the map is from

New England to Virginia. I would be more alarmed to know Gracie is not in this area. Sweetie, we're all in this area, so the map doesn't really show—"

"But it does! Look closer, Miss Foster. See this line?" The dim light of the apartment lamp was just enough for Klara to trace a horizontal line across the drawing of New Jersey. "That's where we can find Gracie."

Nancy tipped the map closer to the lamp. "What's the line, Klara?"

"It's a road. Well, it's probably not exactly a road because I'm not as good with maps as Gracie. She's really a good art—"

A chill from excitement began to run in currents up and down Nancy's bare arms. Her voice quickened in interruption. "Klara, what is the road? What makes you think Gracie is on this road?"

"It goes from here"—Klara again put her finger on the map and traced the line. "See, there's Blair Academy to this place called Andover." Her finger stopped moving.

Time swirled in rushed movement as Klara repeated Gracie's questions about the road. Both woman and girl pulled on their shoes to race out the door and into Nancy's car. The narrow beam of a flashlight lit the map lying across Klara's lap providing direction and hope.

Hours passed and night crossed into the next morning by the time the sporty coupe had driven between Blair Academy and the town of Andover two times. Nancy Foster stopped the car at the edge of a closed gas service station, not caring if she was actually parked or stopped in the middle of the lot. "Klara, I'm afraid our hopes of finding Gracie have failed." She looked at her hands gripping the steering wheel. "We shouldn't have run off without asking for help."

Klara spoke but never stopped staring through the front windshield, worried that if she moved her eyes, she would miss a lone girl wandering in the night. "It's okay, Miss Foster. We tried. We had to move fast or Gracie would be too far away."

Nancy reached for the key on the steering column.

"No! Stop!" Klara clutched her teacher's arm. "What are you doing? Where are you going?"

Sweet understanding poured from the young woman's soft words. "Klara, there's nothing more we can do. We must go back to the academy."

"Then you'll go without me!" Without a plan, Klara reached for the silver handle and pushed against the door. The farther she moved from the car, the faster she walked, going somewhere, anywhere, in search of her friend.

"Klara!" Nancy hurried to catch her young ward, not caring that the car door hung open, letting the dome light send a glow into the dark. "Klara! Please. Wait!" She touched Klara's shoulder just as the young girl spun and collapsed in her teacher's arms unashamed of uncontrollable tears.

"Oh, sweetie, we both want to find Gracie, but we need to think what to do. We might waste valuable time if we continue to drive up and down this road. I'm sure she found someplace to spend the night." Nancy began moving the weeping girl back toward the car, searching the night with her eyes.

Settled back into the coupe, Nancy propped her arm and rested her head against the side window. She tried to think rationally, but her weariness from missing sleep was taking its toll. Her eyes scanned the darkness, leaping among street signs, dark buildings, and occasional car lights bouncing against the night. In the dullness, she read the street signs forward and backward before a glimmer of reasoning passed through her mind. "Klara, exactly where in Andover did you say Gracie was headed?"

"I didn't say." Klara's words moved her to face her helper in the dark. "I didn't say, and I'm not sure she told me exactly."

"Is there some place she knows in Andover?"

"No. Not some *place*. I think it's some *one*. A friend. Theo."

"Theo. Does he have a last name or a house address?"

"No. Just Theo. Well, he probably has a last name, I just don't know what it is. And no"—she shook her head slowly as if a strong shake would shake the memory out of her head—"no, I don't think he lives here."

Nancy sat quietly praying that Klara would talk until some connection to Andover would be clear.

"No, he doesn't live in Andover."

Her long silence caused Nancy to tilt her head to see if Klara had drifted asleep.

Klara's words fell into a mumble. "Oh. Something about boys…a place for boys…mad she couldn't go too…"

"Boys? There's a camp. I've heard about a camp in Andover. I really don't know what they do there, but we're about to find out."

Nancy Foster knew in the quiet dark she would have to locate the city boundaries to find any hint of a camp. She had been to Andover in daylight, but the night distorted what should have been easy roads out of town. The center of town sprawled out in too many directions.

"It's useless to try to find direction in the dark, and I'm running low on gas. For now, we'll stay here at this service station. We'll park for the night and get a little sleep." Nancy patted the hand of her passenger. "We'll find her, Klara. In daylight. I promise."

On the Verge

Cold. Hard. Tethered wrists. Images awakened Gracie's memory in fear of the concrete bed of Hadamar where months earlier she had been tied and unable to stop Viktor Brack from running the cold scalpel over her arm.

"No! No! Please. No!" The chilled thick of nothingness swallowed Gracie's muffled sounds, inviting no one to hear. She begged her eyes to make out detail in the blackness, but only her hands could tell her that she was cocooned inside something metal. She tried to stretch out from where she lay in a ball, but the metal shell kept her cramped.

"Owoh." Gracie tried to move her back away from whatever metal pressed against her spine. In swirling motion of thought spawned by a nightmare, she remembered hands that moved over her, pressing then pounding as her brain awoke the memory of a man forcing her inside the trunk of his car.

Gustav Kaercher's leather dress shoes pounded up the steps and into the empty cabin where leaders had left cold cigarette and cigar ashes in their hurry to set the bund camp into a flurry of activity for the day.

Kaercher twisted around, giving every angle a quick look before he sauntered to a sofa on the back wall. "Not here, eh? Not here to share my good news? Fine then. I'm ready for a good nap, anyway." Scarcely were the words out of his mouth and the leather dress shoes kicked onto the floor before he was snoring in sleep.

"I heard you couldn't stand us havin' all the fun, so you flew in from Germany. Get up, ya old grizzly." A flying clipboard hit the table and skidded to a stop. Leader Gerhard did a quick balance on one leg as he swept the other high enough to kick the end of the sofa. "We heard you were in bund territory, but I thought it was just a vicious rumor."

Kaercher yawned and cracked open one eye just enough to see the silhouette of Gerhard dragging a chair away from the table. "That you, Gerhard? I didn't think you'd get your grimy hands off the assembly line long enough to spend a week training minions." He grunted as he grabbed a pillow to stuff behind his shoulders. "Well, good for you. You either love torture or hate your wife to come spend your vacation out here in the boonies with a bunch of kids."

"Thanks for the compliment and leave my personal life outa this, Gustav. Camp's not over for 'nother half week. Watcha doin' back now? Oh, I know Kuhn said you asked for some kids, but as far as I know, they haven't been trained to…"

Gerhard dug through papers and trash scattered on the table. "Not a lot of excitement around here today." A half grin was interrupted as he inhaled and lit the cigarette he found. "No one will believe the pretty little visitor who got lost on her way to Andover today. Some pretty little lady and her daughter looking for someone named Theo. Too bad I had to tell her there are no campers here by that name. She sure was a lot better to look at than our bunch of camp leaders with scruffy whiskers. Hated to see her drive away, but what would we do with a pretty woman around here?"

"Where is everybody?" Kaercher sat up and looked around, unashamed to hide that he was already bored with the leader's ramblings.

"They're out on duty. I got the job of stayin' here at camp to corral the rats while the others took the fun jobs. Kuhn's got most of the big boys out on a day hike, trying to see if they can survive on plants and fish, I guess, 'cuz I saw a food pack still sittin' on the table in the mess hall when I went for breakfast." The leader burst into a raspy chuckle that ended in a phlegmy cough.

A spit wad hit an empty cup that had been left on the table. "Ugh." Gerhard swiped his mouth with the back of his hand. "Sorry for the interruption. Anyway, as I was sayin', Dan's got six—no wait, seven—seven boys out on one of his concocted survival missions. Trying to see who'll have any guts left to do your service, from what I'm told."

The empty darkness behind Kaercher's eyes picked up a twinkle. His lifeless expression curled into a tight-lipped grin as he lay back down and, with an insolent snore, shut out the other man.

The quiet camp provided a perfect place for a resting robot, but even Murphy became bored from the lack of activity. Robotic sensors kept his nose busy with doglike instinct as he padded around the deserted camp. Theo's command to "roll" into a shiny ball had no importance with no one in camp besides a visitor and a bund leader who were both getting an afternoon nap.

Not even a slight buzz could be heard as Murphy's sensor chip recorded sound, pictures, and even smells of the camp. Yellow transport lights intermittently flashed, but no one noticed the robotic dog. It was three quarters through the day before Murphy wandered to the edge of the camp to lift a programmed leg—though nothing was expelled—against the white-walled tire of a red coupe.

Yellow lights flashed to red with the word *danger* scrolling across Murphy's collar. A sharp noise startled the little dog. He had been warned by his master to stay disguised as a ball and not get caught, but the command failed to compute as the dog's internal programming pulsed across twisted lines of good and bad. Murphy hopped on stiff legs with sharp barks between whimpering howls to both fend off and yet respond to thuds that came from the back of the red Ford.

Gracie lay still inside the trunk of the coupe. *What was that? Who's out there?* It was difficult to recognize sounds from the outside, if indeed, she heard anything at all. Frightened of awakening evil but more frightened of staying trapped, Gracie hit upward against the top of the trunk. "Hey!" A single shout followed the pound. She lay in the dark silence to listen.

Murphy's recharged system was alert, and he heard Gracie's voice. Two front paws began to violently claw against the shiny red trunk.

Something's trying to get in. Gracie shrank back into the dark trunk, unable to understand the sounds. Unmistakably, she heard the sound of Murphy's bark. *Murphy? Is this a trap? How could it be...*

Gracie pressed her face to the metal of the trunk. "Murphy? Murphy?" Her whispers came with unreasonable hope.

Something outside scratched faster and faster as if trying to dig into the metal. Between whispers Gracie strained her ears to listen. Whimpers. She was sure she heard the high pitch of a dog whimpering. Excitedly, Gracie pounded and frantically kicked with her heavy boots. "Murphy! Is that you? Murphy! Help me, Murphy! Go get Theo!"

Pumping both legs with kicks that made no difference against the heavy metal trunk, a foot slipped and kicked against a crunch. Gracie pulled back her foot. She could see her shoe. Daylight penetrated where her foot had kicked against the taillight of the coupe. Murphy's barks came louder.

"Stay back, Murphy! I'm kicking again." Intentionally, the heavy boot was aimed at the taillight that crumpled out of its socket. "Murphy!" Gracie scooted her face to fill where the light had been. A snout poked back with a tongue that licked Gracie's face. "Oh, Murphy. Oh, I love you, buddy. Get help. Murphy, go get Theo!"

Still trapped in the metal cave, Gracie watched as Murphy turned with a whimper and ran back to a row of white tents blocked by the trees that lined the camp.

Theo, come get me. Please, Theo. Listen to Murphy. Come get me. Wringing her bruised hands, she lay back and prayed that Theo would come. Soon.

Murphy ran in and out of the tent several times and even plunged through the wool blanket that covered Theo's cot until half of it hung to the ground. The robotic dog understood the command to find Theo, but without reasoning skills, he was unable to pick up on a scent or scene that would lead him to his master. Noise of boys coming in from their afternoon activities nearly caught Murphy off guard before he rolled into a silver ball tucked behind the wool blan-

RENDERED

ket. An imperceptible seam of the ball cracked to listen for any words that would connect him to Theo.

Over the next several hours an air of disturbance hung over the camp. Leaders shouted more than usual. Boys hurried in and out of the tents more than usual. A roaring bonfire was lit earlier in the evening than usual. Programmed not to think or assume, Murphy lay under the foot of the bunk, aware that something wasn't right but unable to understand. Momentarily, the tent was unoccupied while boys were eating dinner in the mess hall. For Murphy, it was a chance to pace around the inside and outside of the tent in search of his master.

Scuffling noises from the mess hall and the slamming of the wooden screen door were warnings to Murphy to take cover when the boys finished eating. Scarcely had he ditched under the foot of the bed than Theo's bunkmate plopped down with another young boy beside him. Murphy didn't realize the end of his tail lay exposed from under the wool blanket hanging between the two cots.

"Mouse!" A sharp cry came from the neighboring cot and an even sharper pain caused Murphy to yap as a foot stomped down on the tip of Murphy's exposed tail. Squeals from voices that had not yet deepened covered Murphy's telltale yap.

"Kellen! Get off my bed and help me catch it!" Orville's voice rose above the shouts.

Two boys dropped to their knees and nearly knocked heads as they lunged under Theo's cot in search of an elusive rodent.

"Not much stuff for a mouse to hide in down here, just a piece of rope, a comb, and a ball." The two boys sat back from where they had their heads poked under Theo's cot. "C'mon, Kellen. There's no mouse, and I want to talk."

"What's up, Orville?" Kellen sat cross-legged on the cot.

"Something's happened. I'm not sure what, but the leaders have been upset for two days." Orville dropped his voice to a whisper.

"Why? Everything looks okay to me except there's a mouse on the loose in here." Kellen kept his eyes to the ground in case the mouse appeared again.

"I dunno. Leader Dan called a meeting at 1900 hours at the bonfire. We're supposed to stay out of their hair until then." Orville gulped and looked at the cot next to his. "If I see Friedrich, I'll ask him when he gets back. Some of the guys had a wilderness adventure. I don't know how long they're s'posed to be gone. Maybe the older boys know what's up."

Two boys just nodded at each other trying to be fearless campers but struggling to suppress childish fears of the unknown.

"C'mon, Kellen. Let's walk around camp until time for the bonfire."

No other voices could be heard from under the cot where a silver ball lay still, holding a silent robotic dog inside.

Curiosity, boredom, and expectation of new adventure conjoined into a mass of nervousness and giggles as the camp boys congregated around the bonfire.

The cross-armed stance of Director Kuhn standing in the middle of the circle made all laughs and conversations of the campers fade into the evening air.

"Boys, we need an informational meeting. When this meeting is done, you'll all be asked to return to your tents…"

An audible "aww" erupted as the boys reacted to the punishment of being sent to their tents while daylight still filled the sky.

"Enough! We, Leader Dan, Leader Gerhard, and I, have some duty to take care of. The last thing we need is to be chasing a bunch of kids around. We need you to stay put until we tell you to come out of your tents, maybe until morning."

"Aw, c'mon!" A voice from the back spoke out but got suddenly quiet as the director spun on a heel to find the boy who dared to speak against the camp director's demand.

Leader Dan stepped toward the fire in the middle of the circle. "I'll take it from here, Director Kuhn." His voice varied from loud to soft to loud again as he looked around the big-eyed faces.

"Most of you know we had a survival hike two days ago. Seven boys went out. The first day, two returned by dark and three more straggled in during the night. We're waiting for the other two,

RENDERED

expected them to return yesterday. That didn't happen, so tonight we'll keep the fire burning high to help give them direction." He scanned the circle of faces and pointed at two boys in the center who squatted on one knee. "You two"—Leader Dan pointed with two fingers shaping a *V*—"you're in charge of keeping the fire going and going strong until the last ones return." His arm plopped down against his hip. "The rest of you, stay in your tents. When anyone from the wilderness hike returns, we'll ring the bell by the mess hall." A puff of breath—half sigh, half exhaustion—came from Leader Dan before he turned to walk through the circle of boys, not stopping until he shut the wooden door of the leaders' cabin behind him.

"Dismissed," Leader Gerhard spoke one word and sent all but two boys scurrying to their tents in silent obedience.

Between bonfire meeting and lights-out, boys filled the hours with card and dice games. The only interruptions were trips to the latrine and three times when the mess hall bell ticked off a clock's number in each camper's brain.

"Rummy." Kellen systematically stacked his cards while three others tossed their cards to the cot. "Who's still missing?" He spoke words that all boys in the white tent wanted to know but didn't want to confront.

Orville's eyes moved to the next cot. "Friedrich's not back yet. He's tough, guys. He'll be back."

"Yeah, but who else?" A voice of one of the young kids spoke as boys moved flashlights around the darkening tent.

"No one from this tent."

"When I was at the latrine, someone said Günter's still gone."

"Günter?"

"Maybe they killed each other!"

"Stop it! Just stop it right now!" Orville exploded off the cot. "You're all talking like a bunch of little kids! You don't know Friedrich like I do. He's good. Günter's good too. They're smart. They're probably off fishing and really enjoying the hike. That's why they signed up. You'll see. You'll see!"

Kellen picked up the cards and patted Orville on the shoulder. "You're right, Orville. I'm gonna hit the sack. Night, guys."

No more bells rang out before the tent was filled with the rhythmic breathing of sleeping youths. Orville fought sleep as long as he could. He lay on the edge of his cot, fingering Friedrich's charm that hung around his neck, waiting for his friend to return to camp. He, too, succumbed to sleep, letting the driftboard charm dangle from the side of the cot.

Sound sensors stilled, giving Murphy his first chance to resume his search for Theo. He extended his front legs and pulled himself from under the cot, letting his back legs drag in a stretch behind him. He stood in the dark tent between the cots waiting for someone to give him a command.

Though Theo had never shown Murphy the young friend named Orville, there was something about the boy that Murphy liked. Feeling bold in the darkness, Murphy pressed his nose against the cot beside him and gave a sniffing rub with his nose until something caught his attention. The beagle moved nothing but his neck as he extended his snout toward the charm dangling from the side of the bed. Camera sensors popped on from an internal recognition chip. Something belonging to his master dangled in front of him. His master. His to take from a boy he didn't know. As gently as picking up a soft toy, Murphy closed his teeth around the dangling lanyard and began a determined pull backward.

"Uhh," the sleeping boy wrestled against the pull on his neck. Caught between wakefulness and sleep, a hand reached to his neck and tried to stop the tug. Murphy clenched his teeth and backed from his stance between the cots.

"Oww. What's going...ow...who's...stop!" Orville shook off the sleep and opened his eyes to look down the snout of a dog. "What? Hey!" He grabbed the lanyard with one hand and tried to pull back. "Oww. Okay, okay, you're hurting my neck. Where'd you come from?" He reached for the dog whose teeth were clenched around the lanyard.

Orville half fell, half crawled off the cot. "Here, pup. C'mere. I'll play with you, but you gotta let go of my lanyard." He reached behind his neck to loosen the knot that held the strings together, thinking he could better fight the tug with the charm in his hand.

Murphy's pull on the lanyard was a battle for his master, and he wasn't giving in. As soon as the knot loosened, the tug was enough to pull the necklace from Orville's grasp. The feeling of victory in the tug of war made Murphy turn and run from the tent to the only other place he felt protected, the car that held Gracie.

"No! That's mine!" Orville scooted out of the tent and blindly followed the dog past the trees at the edge of the camp.

"Pup! Hey, wait!" Orville stopped and stood speechless at the back of a red car where the dog stood with teeth clenched around the charm, and an arm stuck through a hole where the taillight should be.

"Murphy? Is that you?" The arm swung around, feeling for something solid. Eyeing the boy, Murphy stood on his back legs and let the hand feel his snout until the fingers stopped and slowly wrapped around the lanyard. "What do you have, Murphy?" The voice from the trunk of the car spoke again.

Murphy released his clenched jaw as the hand pulled the lanyard into the trunk.

Orville stood watching, not sure if he should run or throw up.

Suddenly an eye popped to the hole in the trunk. "Murphy, did you get Theo? Theo, are you out there? Who's there? Murphy, you okay?" The voice became stronger. "You better not hurt my dog. I'll hurt you. I can get outa here, you know. Who are you?"

"Uhm-mm." Orville cleared his throat to see if he was trapped in a dream of sleep. "Um. I'm, uh, I was trying to get my charm back from the dog."

"Your charm?"

Orville blinked and shivered at the boldness of the voice in the trunk.

"This isn't your charm. It's Theo's. Where is he? Who are you? He'll kill you, ya know."

"Um, sorry. The charm isn't mine. It belongs to my friend, Friedrich. He asked me to keep it until he gets back to camp. Then the dog—"

135

"Friedrich?" The voice rolled the name around. "Oh, right! Theo! His camp name, Friedrich. Where is he? Are you his friend? Please help me."

The voice was talking so fast. Orville wasn't sure how to respond. "Okay. First, Friedrich is my friend, and he's gone."

A yellow porch light popped against the darkness and shone through the tree line.

Orville dropped his voice to a whisper as he squatted closer to the bumper of the car. "Shh. I think someone's outside. Wait. I'll help you." He glanced down at the dog who sat under the broken taillight and wagged his tail making an arc in the dirt. "Well, I'll try to help. What's your dog's name?"

"Murphy."

"Okay. Murphy." Orville timidly extended his hand to touch the top of the dog's head. He jerked his hand back as the dog plopped to the ground and rolled with his stomach up and his head lolled to the side waiting for a belly rub. Orville started to snicker.

A stick cracked against the ground.

"Shh!" Orville's eyes had adjusted to the dark enough to see a form coming through the trees. He held his face close to the hole in the trunk. "Someone's coming. Don't talk." He wrapped an arm around the dog and pulled him against his chest while backing to lie on the ground under the car. He pulled leaves and dirt in to cover a red glow that came from the dog collar. He didn't understand the dog nor the voice in the trunk, but he knew to get caught would lead to more than a reprimand.

The form stumbled in the dark, hitting against the side of the car. Orville tried not to breathe on the shoes that seemed out of place at camp. They were not the boots the leaders wore. The car door clicked open causing the dome light to pop out of the darkness. Scratches and grunts and sounds of movement came from the car above the boy who rested his head over the snout of the dog to keep him quiet and to quell the lighted collar.

Again the shoes shuffled as the form pulled back from inside the car and lit a cigarette. The door was pushed shut leaving only the red glow of the cigarette visible in the darkness. The form turned, spit, took a drag on the cigarette, then retreated back through the trees.

Orville and Murphy lay still until the yellow glow of the porch light vanished on the other side of the trees. Both boy and dog belly crawled out from under the car.

Orville sat with his back to the car and his head near the hole. "Hey, you okay?"

"As okay as I can be for being starved and locked in a trunk forever."

"Okay. Sorry. Lemme think." Orville ran his hand over the trunk and the bumper of the coupe. "I don't know a way to open the trunk. Um. Is there any tool inside you can use to pound your way out?"

"Yeah. I'm sure I'm lying on something that could make some dents, but I really don't care to make a lot of noise and draw attention."

"Oh yeah. Good call." Orville rose to a squat and moved to the side of the car. "Maybe inside the car. The door didn't make a lot of noise when that guy opened it. Won't hurt to look." Orville opened the door and the dome light sprayed into the darkness. "Augh!" Orville clapped his hand up to the light and pushed a lever at the side until the light popped off again. "Sorry," Orville whispered, not sure if the voice in the trunk understood.

In the dark, Orville's hands rummaged through papers scattered across the back seat. His fingers walked along the crease where the back and bottom cushions met. "Hey, maybe. I remember my dad had a car." Sliding his hand between the cushions, Orville gripped and tugged until the bottom cushion lifted and pulled out of place.

The voice in the trunk came from under the back cushion. "I see your hand. Keep doing whatever you're doing. I can see your hand!"

Orville tugged the heavy bottom cushion braced in place by a metal frame. "If I can remove this cushion, can you squeeze under and come out through the car?"

"Is there any way you can remove the top cushion too?"

"I don't think so. I just remember my dad taking out the bottom cushion when some coins fell out of his pocket one time."

"I can't. I'm trying, but the space is too small for me to slide through. Can you use this?" Gracie handed a crowbar through the opening where the seat had been removed.

Orville pried from several directions before a rivet holding the back cushion broke.

"Okay. Keep doing that. Maybe with the back not so tight it will give as I squeeze under."

Orville didn't know whether to laugh or cry as a head of long curly hair followed by a slender teenager wiggled and pulled until she crouched where a seat once was and hugged a young boy she had never met.

"We gotta get you outa here!"

Stumbling from the car, Gracie pressed the door closed before she pointed to where she would hide in the trees and put the lanyard and charm back into Orville's hand.

"He'll come for you when he returns." Orville picked up a silver ball that lay at his feet and hurried back to his tent beyond the trees.

Unplanned

Boys jumped and screamed in the night wondering if the end of time had come to awaken them from their sleep. Shouting mixed with the gong from the camp bell brought boys and camp leaders surging from tents and cabin.

"What's going on? Who's there?" Fritz Kuhn's rough voice threatened to punish if the clanging bell was a prank.

A teen voice neared the leader in the dark. "It's them, Director Kuhn! I had to go to the latrine and didn't take my flashlight, but I saw him stumble outa those trees carrying Günter on his back. They both just fell to the ground, Director. Honest! I didn't want to leave them, so I rang the bell. Honest, Director. I think they're dead!"

Fritz Kuhn scarcely heard the youth's last words as he stumbled and lurched toward a mass on the ground. His commands were filled with urgent authority. "Stand down, boys! Stand down!"

One frowzy-headed kid automatically lifted an arm and muttered "Heil Hitler" in a confused state of not knowing what to do or say. Boys stood around a mass on the ground staring openmouthed and uncomfortable.

Kuhn reached down for a shoulder to drag the two boys apart just as Leader Dan dropped on his knees beside the mass and called for a flashlight.

"Fritz, it's my boys. Lemme in here." Dan pressed the side of his face down to each face in turn. "They're breathing. Fritz, they're breathing! Stand back! You!" A finger pointed to a boy with a flashlight. "Point that down here."

Murmurs and gasps rolled across the crowd of boys. Orville pushed to the middle of the circle and fell to Theo's side.

"Friedrich! Friedrich! Wake up. Please, wake up!"

"Somebody get this kid back. Someone fetch wet rags." A hand waved in Orville's direction.

A shaking flashlight in the dark night was scarcely enough to see the boys. Dan kept his hands against the necks of both boys as if his own beating heart was transferring life into each of his young campers.

"Hey, he's gonna be fine, kid."

"Are you sure, Leader Dan? Are you sure?" Orville wanted to be brave, but the sight frightened him.

"Sure. Yeah. I'm sure."

The circle of boys breathed quietly while leaders Dan and Kuhn talked quietly over the boys and pressed wet cloths against their foreheads.

Voices bounced in Theo's head until he was conscious enough to realize faces loomed over him. "Drinnn."

"What? We're here Friedrich. What?"

"Wad…wadd…drinn." Theo tried to talk, but his thick tongue couldn't form words.

Leader Dan scarcely had time to bark out an order before two canteens were shoved into the inner circle. Dan cradled first one head then the other pouring and pausing while each young man drank, choked, coughed, and drank again.

"Fine. I'm fine." Theo pointed a finger in Günter's direction. "Fine. Help him. Günter. Leg crushed. Just sleep. I'm fine. Just sleep."

Dan leaned down. "Friedrich, are you injured? Anything hurt? Sure you're okay?" Dan patted Theo's chest. His own heart wanted to burst in pride for whatever this young man had done to survive. At the same time, his heart wanted to scream in anger for being suckered into pushing youth beyond their experience. He couldn't stop the maelstrom of concern and rage, knowing that though someone else assigned his duty, he was responsible for the command.

"Fine. Tired. Help." Again he swung an arm in Günter's direction.

"Rest, Friedrich." Dan's hand rested against Theo's chest. "We'll get your story tomorrow. I'm not sure what happened out there, but I have a feeling you're a hero. Rest for now." Dan rose up on a knee.

RENDERED

"Two of you older boys, get Friedrich to his bunk. Someone open the door to the mess hall and get the light on. We'll move Günter inside. The rest of you go to bed. These boys'll be okay. There's nothing you can do 'til tomorrow. We'll all know more tomorrow."

Two older boys pushed to the inner circle to lift the kid they called Friedrich in a cradle hold then shuffled toward a canvas tent carrying their exhausted campmate. Boys stood unmoving, not wanting to leave the circle.

"Dismissed!" Leader Dan stood and commanded campers who hesitantly turned back to their tents in obedience.

The light in the mess hall disturbed the darkness. An hour later it clicked off after the camp director's car backed to the door where a young man was gently loaded into the back seat and taken away.

Orville was surprised to see the silver ball lying beside his bunkmate. He shivered in the warm night as emotions overwhelmed him. The young camper scooted his cot beside Friedrich's so he could sleep with one hand on his friend's arm, ready to help if needed.

Theo felt the hand on his arm, but his eyes didn't open. "Who's there?"

"It's me, Friedrich. It's me. Orville."

"Who else?"

"No one else, just me. Want me to move that ball off your cot?"

"Ball? Murph." The corner of Theo's mouth tipped into a slight smile, invisible in the dark tent. "No. No. Leave ball..." His voice drifted.

"You gotta rest, Friedrich." Orville leaned his face to the next cot and kept his voice low. "You gotta rest now. I got something to show you, but you gotta rest first."

Theo swallowed the cotton dryness in his throat. "Okay. Res..."

Conversation ended, but the grip on Theo's arm stayed until just before dawn when Orville woke with a feeling of urgency wrapped around his heart.

No one in camp saw when Orville led Friedrich past the camp hedgerow to show him a girl hidden in the trees.

141

No one rang the mess hall bell at the usual time and woke the campers after the night's interruption.

Camp leaders huddled in their cabin trying to make sense of the unplanned.

A young camper cried silently and held a charm that he didn't really understand. A gift, it was the only thing left from an empty space where there once had been a ball, a woolen blanket, and a friend who promised to protect him.

Secrets

A WOOLEN BLANKET COVERED THREE huddled forms after hugs of reunion melted into sleep. Hunger and pain from Theo's head wound submitted to the exhaustion that submerged him in deep sleep. Reluctantly, Gracie rolled out from under the blanket.

"Murphy." Gracie lifted a corner of the blanket. "Murphy," she whispered again.

Leading with his nose, the robotic beagle belly-crawled from under the blanket. Lights on Murphy's collar showed more red than yellow. Gracie knew his sensors were collecting data of smells, sounds, and sights. Confidence built with determination as she pet Murphy and let her eyes adjust to the early morning color of grey.

Shapes beyond the camp's tree line were smeared into blobs of color. A snapping noise drew her eyes to the flagpoles by the mess hall. A German flag? Surely, Theo would tell her about adventures at the camp where he was a spy. A spy in a German camp? Were they the enemy? Gracie was not only confused but frightened. She returned to the hidden nest in the side of the hillside where Orville covered them with the blanket several hours earlier.

"Should we leave?" Gracie tilted her head toward a shoulder so her whisper could drift to the face lying just above her own. "Theo? Are you awake?"

Two arms tightened in a cocoon around Gracie. Her free hand bent at the wrist and patted one arm. "Does that mean we're not leaving?"

"Yep." Another tightening of the arms drew Gracie closer into the body shell of protection. "We're fine. Orville covered our nest… blanket…not find us…"

The next sound was a heavy sigh and deep breaths of sleep. Gracie trusted Theo's judgment and tightened her own body curl around a small dog that lay tucked against her stomach. After her struggles in the trunk of the car, she was willing to rest. She felt comfort in Theo's arms, but the sights of the camp made her uneasy. Would she still be hunted, even in this country? How long would Theo continue to fight for her?

Two days with a night between, the heavy woods sheltered the teens, undetected except by the boy who smuggled food to them. Sixty feet away from their nest the red sedan nosed against the tree line where the grinding start of its engine raced against the pulsing blood in Gracie's temples. She tensed against Theo, still deep in sleep, until long after the sound of the engine and the fallen branches crackling under the tires were covered by distant sounds from camp.

Gracie lay still, straining her ears against the quiet. A cold wetness touched between her nose and lip. "Uuh!" The leafy divot of earth popped as the blanket cover spewed upward where Gracie bolted. Under the wool blanket, a blue collar flashed from a beagle who jumped stiff-legged and ready to attack whatever frightened Gracie.

"You!" Gracie's gruff whisper flung out with an arm that wrapped around Murphy's front legs. "Oh, Murphy! You scared the liver outa me!" A wagging tail and wet nose bumping against Gracie's face assured the crying girl who snuggled back down.

"What time is it?"

"What?" Gracie turned to the form beside her.

"What time...ucht—" Theo's words were cut off by a beagle that jumped over Gracie to land on his master's stomach. "Murphy, nice plant...ugh...not in my face, Murphy!" Ignoring all reprimands, the robotic beagle found no reason to hold back welcoming his master's voice.

"Actually, it's kinda hard to know since we're under this heavy blanket. My guess, from the times I crawled out, we've had at least one day and night go by. Now another day."

"Crawled out? Why'd you leave?" The darkness of their nest didn't show Theo's look of confusion.

"Really? You think my bladder can wait two days?" Gracie chuckled and patted Theo's arm. "Just shows how tired and dehydrated you are. What happened to you, anyway?"

"Umm. Funny. I was about to ask you the same thing." A long arm pushed up on the edge of the blanket where it lay against the earth. "Looks like daylight out there right now." The blanket was set back in place. Again Theo wrapped his arms around Gracie.

"That's a nice, tight hug. It almost makes me forget we're hiding in a hole in the ground."

"It's my safety hug."

"So what exactly is your hug saving me from?" Gracie teased out of curiosity.

"Clouds."

"Aw. But I like clouds. At the academy I'd watch them and pretend they carried me to you."

"No, not the pretty ones that make me think of you too. I'm saving you from the dark clouds." He hugged a little tighter. "Speaking of dark, let's catch up and plan while it's daylight. Orville gave us a pretty good hole-in-the-ground hideout. We can move better in the dark."

"I know. And I know how to get outa here." Gracie's voice had an excited lilt.

"Oh, you do, huh? So you gotta map in your pocket?"

"Actually, yes. Yes, I do." Gracie was anxious to tell Theo about the map she had drawn in Miss Foster's class. She had drawn the road that would take them back to the White House.

Side by side the teens ate food Orville had brought them and made plans to find Gracie's road. They whispered their tales under the blanket and listened to the snoring of a contented and loyal dog.

Report

Breakfast at the White House felt the most like coming home since nearly a year earlier in the home of their German guardian, Jahile Möeller. Warm breads and porridge beckoned sweetly with the aroma of fresh bacon and eggs.

Without being prompted, both teens swiftly stood from their seats at the table as a butler wheeled the president's rattan chair accompanied by the First Lady. Not waiting for formalities to be addressed, Gracie rushed to Mrs. Roosevelt and fell into her warm embrace.

"Oh, children!" The strength of the First Lady's voice and arms sent a welcome vitality into the room. "Oh, oh yes! And Murphy!"

Theo's hands clapped together to call Murphy back to his side but not before the robotic hound clamored around the feet of the kind lady.

Laughter was light and refreshing, even to a stoic commander-in-chief who ordered to be wheeled to the table to "get on with the first order of the day—a hearty breakfast!"

Gracie blushed as a stout woman walked through the door. "Hick! I mean, Miss Hick! Uh, sorry, sorry to lose the clothes you gave me."

A hearty laugh burst from the First Lady's personal secretary. "Gracie, I've laid out another dress for you in your room, but Eleanor suggested a pair of dungarees and a linen shirt may be more to your liking, so they are there too. Choose and wear as you wish, my dear girl. It's more than clothing that makes up a beautiful young lady like you."

After breakfast, Gracie enjoyed the chance to try on and choose from a selection of clothing that had been gathered and left in her room. Indeed, the new dungarees felt good against her legs. Later, she thanked Hick for three outfits without admitting the new wardrobe included a simple pink cotton print dress with matching slippers that made her feel special.

Theo also found new clothes laid out as payment for his services, but his selection was soon tossed beside his new travel bag. For now, he had to figure how to convert intel from Murphy's internal data system into an early twentieth century technology. He turned to the butler who had followed him into the room.

"Excuse me, sir. Would you please tell Henry, ur, Mr. Wallace that I need the services of someone with a camera and someone with a…"—he snapped his fingers as he searched for a word "an, um…oh, a recorder, you know, to copy sound."

The butler tilted his head. "A recorder? Do you mean a Magnetophon?"

Theo gave one final snap with his fingers. "Uh, sure. I mean, yep. Yes. Yes, sir. A magnet-er-other. Um, please. Oh, and someone who can run it!" Theo added as the butler bowed out through the door.

Knowing it would be best to avoid time-travel intricacies, Theo asked for the meetings with the cameraman and the soundman to be held in private. Behind closed doors, a man with a box camera leaned down to focus, snap, readjust, mumble under his breath, and snap again. Theo couldn't understand what the man found so difficult about copying pictures that scrolled across his wrist computer.

Although the man asked how the pictures appeared on what he knew as a watch, Theo guessed more confusion and questions would come if he tried to explain the download from Murphy's internal recording system to the nop. He winked at the photographer as he quipped, "Ask me no questions, and I'll tell you no lies."

As the man with the camera box left the room, a butler waiting in the hall half bowed in a motion to follow. Theo was fascinated as he was escorted to a room with heavily insulated walls to prevent conversations being overheard.

"Wow. Is this some kind of interrogation room? This is cool." Theo started to wander around the small room, wondering how apparatus and machines perched on various tables were used. Murphy skirted the room as an innocent dog, but the flashing yellow collar verified that a sophisticated recording sensor from the future absorbed everything his vision reached.

"Sir." Theo's attention was brought to a man sitting at a small table covered with a large metal box. "Sir, shall we get started? I believe you have a verbal document for me to record. Did you bring it with you?"

Theo's grin was nearly a smirk as he realized a chasm of technology was about to be crossed. "Yeah. Sure. C'mere, Murphy." Theo patted his thigh and sat by the table just as Murphy bounded onto his lap. "Here we go." He smiled at the man's apathetic expression.

The man held out a hand. "Your device?"

Theo laughed. "Well, I don't think you want me to set my dog on your hand."

Any fondness that could have been assumed from the expression on the man's face melted into a clenched jaw. The outstretched hand lowered to the table where it folded with the other hand.

"Aw. I'm sorry. Uh, sir." Theo swallowed his grin. Something in the man's expression reminded him of his twenty-first century history teacher, Mr. Medi, right before a discussion of a missing assignment or a bad grade.

"I, uh, I do find your work in here fascinating, uh, sir." Theo tried his best to get back into good graces with the stoic man or at least to loosen the stern look on his face.

"The device?"

"Yeah. Okay. Well, it's a little different where I come from. The device is actually inside the dog collar."

Not even an eyebrow raised as the dark eyes stared back.

"Okay." Theo squirmed in the wooden chair. "Here. I'll show you. Uh, do you have a screwdriver?"

Minutes later, without explanation, Theo held an earbud beside the microphone that transferred sound from Murphy's collar onto a reel-to-reel magnetic recording tape. He swallowed hard as he listened to bund camp leaders speak freely, unaware that a metal ball under the table absorbed the words that would convict the camps as traitors on America's own soil.

Three hours later, Theo stood with printed pictures from the man with the camera box and a round metal container that held a metal reel of taped conversations from *Hindenburg* to bund camp.

Through many meetings in the next few days and many hearty snacks, Theo and Gracie told of events at the Blair Academy and at the Bund Camp Nordland. Gracie's stories spoke names like Klara and Miss Foster in ways that left tender impressions upon the hearts of all who listened and prompted a generous endowment filtering back into the academy.

The afternoon came when Theo talked of what he understood and didn't understand from the camp. He was blunt about what scared him and the physical struggles that actually saved another camper's life.

"We suspicioned but without proof of how much the enemy tries to infiltrate and destroy from the inside!" White House Advisor Henry Wallace vacillated between anger of Americans turning on their homeland and a sick feeling in the pit of his stomach.

Chairs nestled in a circle on the White House blue carpet held forms of men who sat with stern expressions and little movement save for the pencils that scratched along the notebooks they held. Theo gulped and returned the silent stares until the voice from the rattan wheelchair popped his attention back from an unseen silent hole of space.

"Young man, your stories assure us that we are blessed to have a youth who has adult reconnoitering skills." A smile joined a nod from the president's head. "You have not disappointed us. Nor have you," he added with a plump index finger pointed at Gracie. "Let me reassure you, young man, as you were told when you were first asked to visit the bund camp, all you tell us remains in strict confidence, keeping your identity out of public knowledge." The rattan chair squeaked as the president pressed against an armrest to turn his upper torso and face the man beside him. "You told him, right, Henry?"

"Absolutely, Mr. President. We instructed him that *all* he learned would be divulged to us, and in return, his identity will remain a secret as he returns to his, uh-hum, normal life here in America after the completion of his interrogation."

President Roosevelt raised an eyebrow when Henry Wallace punctuated the word *all*, but swiveled back around in his chair and flipped his hand as if swatting an imaginary fly. "So then, yes, Henry. I believe a simple *yes* is your answer."

"Yes, Mr. President."

One corner of Theo's lips turned upward at the president's control of the room. Now he was comfortable, even though he knew he would hedge a little and explain a lot. It was time to bring the future under the noses of the 1937 government men assembled in the room.

"Mr. President, sirs"—Theo nodded around the room before he gave a quick double pat to his thigh—"Murphy."

In a comical twist from lying silently beside Gracie's feet, Murphy spun and jumped to stand, facing his master with all four legs stiff and his tail wagging. His quick appearance into the circle caught one government man off guard, causing him to let out an exclamation that led into a volley of chuckles from the men and a hearty bellow from the president. Murphy registered the laughter as good and took several more stiff-legged pearl hops in a circle before Theo reached down and placed a hand on the dog's back.

"That's good, boy. Sit."

Tension in the room snapped, and Theo knew Murphy had paved the way for a joining of two worlds. "This, my friends, is my dog, Murphy. He's a…" Theo paused, remembering how he had mentally practiced his speech of Murphy's role in the spy mission. "Well, let's just say, he's a good companion, and if you don't mind, I think I'd rather keep on the topic of the bund camp and not how Murphy helped me gather information."

Theo averted his eyes from curious stares by digging into a portfolio he held in his lap. "I'm not sure what at the camp would interest you, so I'll just share some pictures and with the help of my new friend"—he brazenly winked at the man from the recording room—"a little sound." He handed the reel to be placed on a reel-to-reel projection device.

The Magnetophon had scarcely clicked off before President Roosevelt punched out a "Thank you!" and a gesture to one of the government men. "David, please escort these two youths to the door." The president smiled warmly as he looked directly at Theo and then Gracie. "We're finished for now, and we thank you for your service."

Theo was pretty sure no one in the room breathed as he, Gracie, and Murphy obediently went to the door that closed quickly and solidly behind them.

Discovery

AFTER SEVERAL DAYS OF BLAIR Academy and Bund Camp Nordland reports to the White House staff were adequately completed, Theo and Gracie were anxious to fill days exploring. They knew they'd miss the attention and care given by the White House staff, but they were free to go with the promise that they'd keep in touch. Henry Wallace fulfilled an earlier promise to point the way to a quiet place called Menlo Park, once used by two scientists from Theo's ancient past, Thomas Edison and Nikola Tesla. Before they headed north, Eleanor Roosevelt promised a fresh meal and a place to sleep when they returned to 1600 Pennsylvania Avenue.

"Amazing." The word came in a whisper as Theo held Gracie's hand and stepped inside the dilapidated building. Murphy crowded through the doorway adding the click of his paws against the dusty wood floor.

The wide-eyed stare squeezed against the frown lines on Gracie's forehead as she looked around the stale room. "No one's been here for quite some time, and I'm not sure we should be here now." Almost against her will, her feet continued to shuffle behind Theo as he walked from table to table. "That sign on the door said do not enter. Theo, what does *condameend* mean?"

"It means you didn't read very well. The sign says *condemned*." Theo gave a half-hearted response without interrupting his eyes as they panned the room.

"Okay, smarty-pants. So what does *condemned* mean?" Gracie unintentionally bumped a table causing a beaker to topple and roll to the floor where it became nothing more than shattered glass.

Murphy let out a sharp bark and jumped in a circle as if the beaker were attacking them from behind.

"Oops. Sorry, Murphy." Gracie looked down at the glass shards.

Theo stopped his walking and panning long enough to face Gracie and put his hands on her shoulders. "First, it means we're not supposed to be in here because someone wants to tear it down or let it fall down. Second, it means we need to be careful because we don't want to break what they plan to destroy!"

Gracie's furrowed brow tipped at him and softened when he planted a quick kiss in the middle of her forehead.

"Actually, I'm not sure why we're in here, but this place is amazing." Theo released her shoulders and turned to walk farther into the room. "It may connect us back to my world. Be careful."

With a sigh meant to be heard, Gracie crossed her arms and leaned against the table that once held the beaker. "You're not making a lot of sense right now."

"Unbelievable."

"Okay," Gracie lightly quipped. "You're making a lot of unbelievable sense right now."

"Would ya look at that." Theo lifted an arm and pointed at a cylinder on a table. "A Tesla coil!"

"A what? That round metal thing?" Gracie only glanced where Theo was pointing before she started some of her own looking out of curiosity.

Murphy jumped from chair to table and stood with his neck pushed as far forward toward the coil as he could without falling over. Theo ran his hand from Murphy's head to tail.

"Probably harmless after sitting for who knows how long, but if I get that thing charged, we may light up your face whiskers if we're not careful." Theo gave a pat as Murphy lay down with his nose still pointed toward the coil.

"I wonder if there's an electric current to this building." Theo twirled in place looking at the walls until he remembered the eerie lights that hung from the ceiling in Germany's chamber of horrors called Hadamar. "If I just knew more about what they did and didn't have in 1937…" Theo let his words drift away with his thoughts.

"Aha! Look, Murph!" Theo pointed above the table where a bulb hung from a fixture with an electrical outlet. "Electricity. We'll connect the Tesla coil and see what gases we can get to move. No one's using this old building. It can be our base, our home for now. It'll sure beat sleeping in the woods. C'mon, Gracie. Let's camp out here for a while. This'll be fun!"

"Fun?" Gracie's voice rose in pitch and volume. "What are you saying? I thought we were on another mission to explore, and you want to stop and have fun?" Gracie turned with her arms crossed to express that she was not having fun.

Theo put a hand across her thin arms where they were crossed. "Zikes, Gracie. I'm not offtrack of why we're here. Really. It's just that seeing all of this science stuff"—he turned and gave a waving gesticulation in a wide arc—"it reminds me of home." He looked back at the emotionless face of the beautiful girl. "It's what I love to do, Gracie. It's science. Wrapped up in every coil and tube and dust particle in here is an imaginary cord that ties me back to my dad." Theo looked around the room. "Funny, Gracie, but this whole time jump has made me realize what I want to do with my life." He stopped long enough to look at Gracie's dark eyes. "I want to be a scientist. I want to be like my dad."

The corners of Gracie's lips turned upward, and her crossed arms broke as she put a hand on Theo's chest. "You know, I guess we're still learning about each other. I knew your dad was responsible for building the machine that made you jump backward through time, but I guess I never thought about him being a real scientist."

Theo didn't know why, but in the dust-filled shack, he pulled her into his arms for a hug that had no rush and no plan.

"So what's your dad's job?"

"He's a *Kartograph*." The whispered response tugged at memories. She broke the silence that followed. "He drew maps."

"No kidding! Wow! I'm like my dad, but I think you must be a lot like your dad too!" Theo's arms wrapped the hug a little tighter.

"Why do you say that?"

"Well, I've only heard about one map you've drawn, but you did get us from the bund camp to the White House." Theo paused to

RENDERED

brush his fingers through the curls that framed Gracie's face. "Don't think I'll ever forget how you sensed the surroundings in those German cities and even when we were lost in the forest after we... after we—" A knot plugged Theo's thought path from his brain to his voice.

"After we left Hadamar?" Gracie leaned her head back enough to see a face that looked as if he were recalling a bad dream. She snuggled back against his chest allowing his arms to lock around her.

"That makes a lot more sense."

"What does?"

"You said your mom left in the middle of the night. Where'd she go?" Theo's questioning voice was filled with more than curiosity.

"I don't know. Herr Möeller told me that she and another woman left Germany to find the border of Austria where Papa would meet them." Gracie tried to think where Theo's question would lead.

"Right. Did you ever wonder how they would know where to travel when they were surrounded by the Third Reich that wanted every Jew, and in your mom's case, every Romani—every gypsy—to be killed?" Theo ran one hand from the top of Gracie's head down her soft curls to where they lay against her back. "He made a map for her, didn't he? That wasn't a last-minute plan. They knew what they needed to do. He mapped for her a way of escape."

A soft noise came from the face pressed against Theo's chest.

"Remember how you told me he loved her? He really was her knight. He protected her even when they were apart. He mapped her path to safety." Theo's voice tightened with emotion. "He saved her. If she followed his map, Gracie, she lives. I just know it. She's alive, and your Papa would know where to find her. They live, Gracie. I just know it. They live."

Silence was soft in the air of the dilapidated building, underscored with the undulating sound of a soft cry.

Neither youth counted the minutes that passed until Theo held Gracie away with his large hands on her shoulders. "We can do this, Gracie. For our parents, we can do this mission!" He walked to the table where the cylinder wrapped with a metal coil stood dusty and lacking use. "This coil was invented by a scientist named Nikola Tesla. He studied how gases react to a coil when electricity is connected." He pointed to the base of the coiled cylinder. "See when power goes through the capacitor which soaks up the charge until it can arc across this gap…" Theo caught a glance of Gracie's blank stare.

"I don't know or even think I care what you just said. Sorry." Gracie raised her eyebrows.

"Aw, that's okay. The important thing is that maybe I can use this to connect back to IRIS and home. At least it should help. My dad plans to get us back to the future. Maybe ol' Tesla here can help." Theo ran his hand up and down the dusty coil.

Gracie's expression was not hiding the worry in her heart.

"It'll be fine, Gracie. You'll see. We'll have a great life back where I belong, where we can belong." He sighed. "Just give me some time to experiment. I've got to see what I can do."

Gracie smiled. "Well, we're not exactly wanted where we are now, so I guess either your science or my map making will need to get us outa here."

Rendered

Not even a breath of wind gave the leaves a dance in the dusk. Murphy followed closely beside Theo's ankle, letting his robotic nose hover slightly above the ground. Theo pushed his hands into the pockets of his jacket. He wasn't cold in the late summer days that had begun to cool, but his fisted hands reflected his unsteady soul wrestling between calm and anxiety.

"Hey, Murph, let's go in here. We have time. Gracie's out exploring on her own until we meet back at the shack for supper." Theo pointed a finger toward a chain-link gate. "There's no sign that says *Keep Out*." He pushed against the spring-loaded gate, allowing enough space to pass through. "Seems like a thousand years since I pushed through a gate like this. Remember, Murph? Back home where I practiced my driftboard tricks at that deserted industrial site." He rubbed the small of his back. "Ugh. I can almost still feel the bruises from all of my tricks that ended in a crash. All part of the learnin' I guess. C'mon, Murphy. You don't want this gate to snap shut before you get…" His words were clipped short as his eyes involuntarily looked down at the pavement.

"Did you see that?" Theo spoke more to himself than to the dog sniffing in wild zigzags.

Theo closed the gate, giving in to the pull of the spring. His head jerked sideways. He was certain something familiar caught his eye, but he never saw proof of the image taunting his mind.

"I know I saw it." Theo slowly shook his head and reached out to touch the gate. "It was so real."

The voice of his master caused a momentary pause long enough for Murphy to look up where the young man spun in a slow circle.

"Murphy, was that in my head? I know I saw a driftboard. No, not just a driftboard. It was *my* driftboard, my VX-3000! Man, I've hardly thought of it since we time jumped, but I know I saw it. I just know it! This place is playing tricks with my memory."

A sigh, sad yet resigned, punctuated the thought of yet another vision that Theo could not explain.

"Murph! Hey, Murphy! Where are you?"

The robotic dog emerged from bushes that lined the drive. "You're going to wear out that sniffer of yours if you keep trotting with it so close to the ground." Theo squatted to pet the beagle that stopped long enough to prop his front paws on his master's leg.

"I had another vision, Murph. At least this one wasn't bad." Theo's eyes scanned the lawn and stone buildings in front of him. "Strange. I've never seen this place. These buildings look kinda new." A long exhale came as his eyes moved slowly across the horizon. "But there's something familiar about..."

The wind picked up, bringing an odious smell. Theo gave Murphy a firm pat and jumped to his feet in one motion. He grimaced, trying to reject the smell of evil that hung in the air.

"C'mon, Murph. Let's get outa here."

Theo pulled open the gate, nearly tripping over the beagle backing through the opening with teeth clenched in a threatening growl.

Unashamed to turn from danger, Theo and Murphy ran. Air, once crisp with nature's scents, was now heavy with a smothering stench that signaled the presence of a jaeger.

"Gracie, be careful." Theo slammed the door behind him and crossed the room to stand across a worktable from his friend. For the two teens, the shack at Menlo Park had become lab and makeshift home.

"Excuse me?"

"Be careful."

Gracie jerked a knob to quench the fire under a beaker where she was heating copper sulfate just to watch the beautiful colors appear in the flame. "I'm not a child who needs to be told how to handle fire and glass." She turned to walk away.

"What?" Theo looked at the apparatus on the table. "Oh," he scooted around the table until he could touch Gracie's shoulder. "No, no! I'm sorry. I really wasn't even thinking about anything here in the lab." Unprompted by any words, Theo wrapped both arms around her.

"Mmstoff. Yphr smmffring me."

Theo kissed the top of the head that pulled back from his chest. "What?"

"You're smothering me! What's with you? First, you scold me to be careful. Then you plant my face against your chest until I can't breathe. I thought girls were supposed to be confusing, but I really can't figure you out right now." Gracie put her hands on Theo's chest and pushed back enough to see his face looming over her.

"I did? I didn't scold, uh, I am? I didn't try to, I mean, I didn't want to smother you. I tried to hug you. That's all."

"That's all? Then why did you walk in here and start bossing me about being careful?"

Theo pulled Gracie back to his chest and gave a gentle hug before dropping his hands to hold hers. "Sorry. I didn't mean to be confusing. Being careful really has nothing to do with the lab. Back home, my dad always let me experiment in the lab. It wouldn't be fair if I didn't let you do a little experimenting too." He turned and walked to a half-darkened window that had once been fully silvered to prevent outside eyes from seeing into the lab.

"It's not safe here."

"What are you talking about? I thought you left that jerk kid back at the bund camp. Why would anyone—"

Theo interrupted in a rough whisper. "Jaegers, Gracie."

"No, Theo. Hitler's evil of the Reich can't get us. We're in America. That can't be." Gracie wanted her brave words to bolster the panic creeping around her heart.

"That's what I believed, until this morning. I was outside of town at some kind of factory, and I smelled one."

"Maybe it was just a smelly vapor from a smokestack or…" No more words were needed. She didn't want to accept the fearful truth as Theo shook his head. "But we killed it."

"We killed one jaeger on the *Hindenburg*. Who knows how many were on that flight or maybe even on other flights or maybe even were already here. I don't know how or why. I just know I smelled one. Murphy smelled it too. Gracie, that's a smell that can't be forgotten."

Gracie hugged her arms across her chest to stop a shiver. "So, what do we do now?"

Again Theo pulled his tiny friend into his arms. "I don't know. I really don't know."

Murphy's low growl and red blinking collar passed unnoticed while the young couple embraced in the old laboratory.

"So what exactly are we doing here? Even with all of the dust, I like watching you fiddle with all of those wire things, but nothing looks like it can get us back home." Gracie's voice dropped. "Wherever that is."

Theo's long legs kicked and pulled as he dragged himself out from under a table where he had been tugging at cords. "Huh?" He looked at the wires in his hands. "I really don't understand these things. Dad had tons of cords in his lab, but they didn't have copper wires inside. The casings in the lab let thin fiber optics transfer without being interrupted by Dad's experiments. Most transfers were in the air."

"That doesn't even make sense. Wires were in the air?"

"No. What we call wires are basically infrared power transfers, usually only in science labs to be able to see the experiments. In life outside the lab, we don't need to see. We'd go crazy if we saw all that's happening in cyberspace." He caught Gracie's expression of confusion. "You know, the airwaves."

"So you're saying power is in the air and is invisible."

"Yeah. Basically."

"I don't believe you. Thanks for the fairy tale."

"Whatever. How did people ever get anything done with all of these tubes with wires inside? I'd be tripping all over the place." Theo looked at the lifeless wire in his hands. "Anyway, uh, what were you saying?"

Gracie grunted and shook her head. "It's a good thing you're so smart because sometimes you talk like a real *Dummkopf*."

Theo jumped at Gracie with a pretend tackle. "Hey, little lady! You think I don't understand some German!"

Gracie struggled against Theo's fingers pressing into her ribs. "Okay, okay, stop with the *Kitzeln*!"

"The kissing?" Theo's lips dove into Gracie's neck.

The wiggling girl burst into giggles. "Not kissing! I said *tickles*! Obviously, you don't know *all* German!"

Their playfulness was all Murphy needed to distract him from his awareness of danger. With a running leap onto a table, he was able to jump between the teens and into the middle of their arms and breaths of laughter until all three collapsed onto the dusty floor.

"Man, I'm hungry." Gracie was the first to pull out of the dogpile. "Do we have any food stash in here?"

Theo rubbed his stomach. "Now that you mention it, I guess we got so busy messing around that I forgot the time. I wish we were closer to sneak back to the Capitol." He pulled himself up. "Lemme finish what I'm doing, and we'll go out to see what that last town's café can feed us."

"Okay. 'Til you're ready, I'll walk around outside. There may still be blackberries on the bushes at the edge of the woods." Gracie shut the door to the shack before Murphy could follow. Though programmed without feelings, the beagle collapsed on the floor with his snout resting on his paws and his eyes on the crack of the door.

Theo kicked at the wires he had pulled from under the worktable. "Useless." He huffed under his breath. "Both the wires and my science." The Tesla coil stood like a sentry keeping watch over the wooden table. Theo traced the coil with a finger.

"Should be some way you can work. Ugh. My stomach is beginning to talk louder than my brain. Later, Tesla. Keep your secret for now. I'll figure a way to get us back home to the future."

Theo turned to the dog on the floor. "Did you hear that, Murph? How weird is that? I'm talking about home as if it's some way-off time and place." He glanced through the half-silvered window. "Whaddaya say we go look for Gra—"

His words were interrupted as Murphy's collar turned a full blinking red with danger lights. Murphy jumped to his feet with barks and growls that could threaten the devil himself.

Before another breath could keep up with his pounding heart, Theo threw open the door, running to follow Murphy's barks and full-speed run into the nearby darkening forest.

"Gracie! Gracie! Where are you? Gracie!" Theo knew Murphy's alarm could not be ignored.

Neither youth nor robot from the future heard their friend's scream and the gurgle that bubbled from her throat.

Stiff legged, Murphy stopped and bounced in a small circle. His computer tracking sensor spun like a compass that had lost its reading.

"Wait. Murph! Wait. Lemme connect to your heat sensor." His leg muscles tightened and told him to keep running. "Zikes! IRIS always did this for me." Theo pounded on his wrist computer. "Augh! Stupid past! Murph! I can't connect my nop. How did these people exist!" He hit the black screen on his arm. "What now, Murph?"

Ignoring his master, Murphy planted his nose into the green-and-yellow foliage. Theo dropped to his knees. "What the heck is going on with your collar?" He noticed when Murphy moved in one direction, the collar lit up full red with the word *danger* flashing on the display, but when Murphy snorted from his olfactory chip, the lights intermittently blinked from full red to sudden black. Red flashes became a little dimmer with each blink of change. The dimming red mixed with Murphy's barks that changed to a sad whimper.

"I dunno why, Murph, but my gut says we need to go this way." Theo's finger pointed in the direction that mixed the red and black lights of Murphy's collar.

Both young man and dog stepped half hurried, half hesitant through the forest until a threatening bark changed to a sharp, wounded cry. Murphy bounded to a body lying on the forest floor.

Theo lunged toward Gracie's body, scooping her into his arms. Her head rolled until long curls dropped to the side, exposing a long screwdriver plunged through the front of her neck with the shaft sticking out the back where ribbons of blood ran red on her beautiful skin.

As if pulling the screwdriver would pull life back into Gracie, Theo yanked and looked at the tool, so similar to one that Gracie had used to escape from a jaeger on the *Hindenburg*.

Cries from Theo's heart and the howls of a dog rose above the trees while Theo, Murphy, and Gracie nested together beside the misused and fatal instrument tossed into a bloody mass of leaves.

Severed

THEO CRADLED GRACIE IN HIS arms and carried her in a half run toward the highway. The pain of loss felt as if the jaeger had clawed Theo's insides. Anger and disbelief poured from his soul in endless tears.

He feared no one would stop, but this was a time gone by when people stopped for a need along the road. Several cars stopped at first with one person after another trying to help, to offer a blanket, to offer advice. Most shivered and looked over their shoulders even though Theo repeated over and over how evil had killed her in the deep woods, too cowardly to show his face. Many shook heads and returned to their cars to pull away slowly and continue on their journeys, unsure of what to do as they had come too late.

Eventually, someone laid a Bible across the space between Theo's arm and Gracie's body. An arm covered in a cotton dress shirt moved a hand to touch Gracie's cheek as a voice whispered a prayer.

"Father of all hope, power, and comfort, we give you this young soul and ask for forgiveness of all. Amen." Only a sigh followed until the man in the cotton shirt urged, "Come now, son. I'll take you where you need to go."

With strength, the arm wrapped around Theo to support and lift while two other men helped raise the lifeless girl without taking her from his arms. One form in motion, a mass of cotton dress shirt, men, and cradled body moved to a waiting sedan. A small beagle trotted along with his snout pointed up toward bouncing soft curls that hung over Theo's arm.

Horror and shock filled the rooms where White House staff spread the news. Theo still sat with Gracie in his arms as Eleanor

RENDERED

Roosevelt and Hicks rushed into the foyer. He could think of no words but looked through blurred vision as the two strong women dropped to their knees in front of him and wept unashamed.

Theo's wishes to bury Gracie in the churchyard of a small town near Menlo Park were granted with a procession of people he recognized and people from the Capitol whom he had never met. Even the rattan wheelchair was rolled across the grasses of the cemetery. The man in the cotton dress shirt returned and offered the last rites with words from the Bible and a prayer.

The Roosevelts ordered a stone with Gracie's name and promised to see that it would be placed at the head of her grave. Though they begged Theo to return with them to the White House and stay a few days, President Roosevelt shook Theo's hand and Eleanor touched his cheek with her soft-gloved hand before they returned to the car without him.

Blankly, Theo turned back toward the grave and saw a young woman and a girl who looked Gracie's age. They held each other and wept before dropping two yellow roses onto the loose dirt. The girl looked up at Theo. "You must be Gracie's friend in the clouds. I'm Klara. I know you don't need to be told, but I want to say, she loved you."

The girl stood on tiptoe to press a kiss onto Theo's cheek before she and the woman walked away.

Alone with his robotic companion, Theo walked to Gracie's grave and fell to his knees, wracked with the pain of loss. Overhead, a silent wispy cloud intercepted a sunbeam as a gentle white feather floated to the earth.

Part III
America, 20—

Transport

Exhausted, Theo pounded his fist on the wooden table.

Murphy jumped onto the old table and pressed his snout into Theo's chest. The dog's impassive robotic wiring couldn't detect his master's anger and frustration, but he knew his master needed a friend.

A hand planted across Murphy's back and gave a quick squeeze before a continuous stroking caused him to sway his back and lift his snout into the air.

"Aw, Murph. It's just not gonna work. I don't even know what to do next. I'm not my dad. I'm not a scientist." He glanced at his hand as he petted Murphy. "I'm not even a scrawny kid anymore. I'm just, just…" Theo didn't want to say the word he felt. The word that ballooned inside him until he was sure it would choke him. He picked up Murphy and cradled the dog in his arms. "I'm just lonely, Murphy. I just want to go home. Just go home." The word *home* caught in the folds of his deep voice.

A flash of blinding light emitted from the Tesla coil. Theo ducked backward and lifted his hand to shield his eyes. Murphy snuggled deeper against his chest.

"Zikes! Now something's interfering with the stupid coil. C'mon…" Theo waved a hand around the metal column of spiraled metal. "Don't mess with me."

A hum came from the gentle glow. He shrugged his shoulders to recenter his backpack that had fallen to the side when he drew back from the burst of light. He squinted and stared at the coil. He'd be prepared for another flash this time. He hoped the piercing light hadn't damaged his retinas. Again a bright flash twisted into a cylindrical form causing him to jerk his arm to cover his eyes. Just as quickly as the light twisted, it vanished and the buzzing coil lost all but a dim glow. A dark form took shape in the dim background of the shack.

"You better not be shorting out on me." Theo squinted into the darkness. "What's that? Murph? You see that shadow? This could be bad, Murph. Roll!" He dropped the silver ball into his backpack. Prepared to run, he glanced around the room wondering if the dark form was blindness from the flash or evil returning. No sound filled the air—not a breath, not a creak of a floorboard. Only silence hung around the dim Tesla coil and the dark form.

Theo turned back to the coil. The dark spot grew behind the coil like a black balloon. The middle of the balloon shape grayed against the blackness and formed into a face. He stared at the smoky vision taking shape. It was the face of a man. A face staring back.

"Dad?" He stared not wanting to blink. "Dad? I've had lots of precognitions in my sleep, but this is weird." The face of Luke Marshall was clear and growing inside the balloon shape of black.

"Dad!" Theo shouted at the balloon. "Dad! I see your face. Dad!"

The balloon vanished, leaving Theo drenched in darkness.

"No! No! Don't do this. Dad! Come back." The young man spun around begging his eyes to see the face of his dad in the darkness. "Come back!"

"Theo?"

He grabbed the straps holding his pack and spun back around ready to stand against whoever, whatever was coming out of the darkness calling his name. The face, the black balloon, the Tesla coil, all were gone. Theo saw nothing, nothing but silvery blue. He stepped into the nothingness with fists clenched, ready to fight.

"Theo?" The voice questioned then grew strong.

"Theodore!"

Theo jerked his head to the sound. The silvery blue pushed toward him in the shape of a man. "Dad?" His dry mouth hung open. "What's happening?" He spoke in a rough whisper not wanting to pop the vision. "Dad?"

"Welcome home, son. Looks like I just missed your birthday."

Murphy jumped out of the open flap of the backpack with a wild sniffing. His collar lit up as sensory receptors bounced.

"Dad? I don't get it. Where are we?" Theo spun in a circle. "Are you real? Am I home? How'd I get here?"

Luke Marshall tugged at his scruffy chin. "Well, I'm not absolutely sure, but I think it has to do with the computer chip we had inserted under your skin." Luke tapped his chest just above his heart. "Here, right after you were born."

"My coordinates chip?" Theo lifted his hand over his heart. "Did the latitude and longitude of our house make me time jump? How? Where's the machine? If I jumped, it didn't hurt. I can't believe it! Am I really home?"

A smile appeared in Luke's whiskers. "Well, first, I'd been tinkering with the idea of using the magnetism of the coordinates to connect with you. It's one thing to move through space, but that's asking a lot of science to move through time. The coordinate force just didn't seem to be enough. Then I realized you had Murphy."

Dr. Luke Marshall pointed at the beagle still sweeping the room with his nose. Murphy paused and raised his eyes to Theo when he heard his name then went back to sniffing.

Luke continued, "At least I hoped you still had him. I also hoped that if I set coordinates in Murphy's collar—simple computer programming—if you had Murphy with you, the force would be stronger."

"Yeah, I had him all right." Theo interrupted his dad. "I was frustrated and holding Murphy and having what mom used to call *a pity party*. What'd you do? How did you make me come home?"

"Theodore, I didn't *make* you come here. Home is a place where you want to be. Just curious, were you trying to come home?"

"Well, yeah, but I'd been tinkering with a Tesla coil—"

"Tesla coil? What in the world! Sorry, go on…"

Theo gave a chuckle at his dad's scientific passion. "Yeah, long story, but anyway, the coil wasn't working. I'd given up. I didn't do anything." He shrugged and held his hands out from his sides.

"Theodore, were you thinking about home?" Dr. Marshall sounded hopeful like he did when he solved a hypothesis.

"I wasn't thinking anything except that I was mad at the coil. I was lonely. I was..." Theo looked at his dad as his voice lifted. "Actually, I think I did say that I wanted to come home." Theo reared back his head in a man's laugh. "Kinda like Dorothy in *The Wizard of Oz*, huh?"

Luke Marshall's eyes narrowed. "The mind God gave you is more powerful than science can harness or understand, Theo."

Both men laughed as pent-up emotions began to surface. Luke slapped his knees and pressed against the armrests of the chair where he sat. "Enough science, Theodore! I lost you to my obsession with science once. I'm not going to miss another opportunity to be with my son."

Luke stood and, with a slight sway, took a step toward his son.

"Dad! Dad, you're standing, you're walking! I thought you were paralyzed from the lab explosion!" Theo's surprise came out in bursts of shouting.

"Well, we scientists have to learn that only God is the Creator. We can take what he's created and work with the brains he's given us to do amazing things." He lifted the bottom of his shirt and patted his waist. "This band is connected to prosthetic sleeves that I pull over my legs. The sleeves give me new legs connected through..." Luke looked up at his son.

"No." Luke shook his head and took steps toward Theo. "No. There's time later for all of that." He lifted both arms toward his son as he walked across the room. "Welcome home."

Home

Nearly five years had passed since Theo followed Viktor Brack back in time to Nazi Germany. Three years had passed since an odious German Reich had sought out and killed Gracie, though her beauty, spirited ways, and love for family had not faded from Theo's heart and memory. Three years had passed since Luke Marshall welcomed his son back home into the future. Time had passed, but so much never changed. IRIS still gave her commands and took care of domestic duties. Luke Marshall still loved the science that went beyond textbook reasoning.

Content to be back to 20— and all he knew as America, Theo had a new desire to explore the states and hike the trails that ran through the forests of New Jersey, searching for answers, absorbing memories.

His heart settled. Finally, he came home.

Theo couldn't ignore the desire to open the door of the front closet. Still leaning in the corner as if waiting for someone to pick it up and pump start the jet, the VX-3000 was propped, ready for use. Theo smirked at the driftboard—"Not today. I don't feel like being dumped in front of pretty girls in the park anymore"—and shut the closet door.

The walk to his dad's lab was planned, but he felt no hurry.

Half a block from an abandoned industrial park, Murphy took off in a run and stopped only to shove his nose through the links of a gate in the property fence. Theo laughed when he caught up to the tail that wagged so hard and fast that it made Murphy bounce in place.

"Really? Really, Murphy? You remember this place?" Theo shoved the spring-loaded gate enough to go through with Murphy at his heels. He shivered with a feeling that he had stood in that same place, but a vision in his memory showed a new industrial building where a dilapidated ruin now waited to be torn down. He shrugged his shoulders to shake the shiver and the memory.

"Yep. I seem to remember some failed driftboard tricks in that old building over there." Murphy watched the hand that pointed and took it as a command to run to the place where steps had crumbled and walls had fallen. Theo peered into the dark of the fallen building. "Can you believe that, Murphy! I don't think anyone has moved the stacks of boxes and crates since I left here five years ago! Huh. So much for progress."

"C'mon, Murphy. There's one more place I need to go before we stop at Dad's lab."

With a snort, though he kept his nose to the ground, Murphy swiveled back toward the gate. There was something good about this place that crumbled and served no purpose but to be an eyesore. Murphy's tail flicked more than wagged, and Theo fell into kicking rocks along the sidewalk as if he were a kid again. He looked back over his shoulder and subconsciously put his hand against his neck where his driftboard charm once hung. Yes. This place was good. It was the memory of childhood and teen years untouched by the brutal horrors of the world. The gate snapped shut behind them while life spun forward.

"I've always been amazed how green a cemetery can be, Murphy. I never see anyone painting the grass like in most neighborhoods." Theo walked with his hands in his pockets and looked around at the green flatland sprinkled with white and gray stones. "Maybe it's the last ditch effort of the people buried here to leave behind a natural beauty so we'll remember them."

The young man walked deliberately, filled with emotion though the robotic dog beside his ankle had been programmed without a heart and soul.

"Here she is." Theo dropped to his knees and patted the green that edged a white granite stone. He traced the letters with a finger.

Beloved Wife and Mother 2010–2044

A sigh filled the momentary silence. "Miss you, Mom. Love you still."

White clouds swirled through the fresh air that encouraged Theo to close his eyes and tilt back his head. Swirls of scent relaxed him. "Mmm. Don't you think we could stay here all day, Murphy?" Theo opened his eyes wondering where his curious robot had gone.

"Murph! Murphy! Where'd ya go?" A soft whistle was answered by a yap across the graveyard.

"There you are." Theo smiled and sauntered to the back of the graveyard where stones sat at angles and tilted in ground that had settled over time. "What brings you back here? Did ya find a fuzzy squirrel to chase?"

The dog glanced up at Theo, then twisted his snout on the ground until he flipped to his back. Tail wagging, feet kicking in the air, Murphy's mouth almost looked like a smile between flapping ears and upside-down jowls hanging loose to expose his teeth. He wiggled his body back and forth as if the earth gave him a most satisfying back rub.

"Hey, buddy. Does this old grass feel pretty good?" Theo squatted down to reward Murphy with a tummy rub. He looked down the crooked aisle and back again. "Man, this area looks ancient." He stopped Murphy's belly rub to reach for the nearest stone. "This is hardly a marker at all. Just a flat stone with a name I can hardly read." Theo put his hand on the stone to brush away a white feather and trace the etching. G-R-A-C..."

Theo crawled to the stone. "Year, what year…1921 to 1937." His heart began to race. "Are you really here? G-R-A-C-I-E. Oh, my dear, dear Gracie! It's you! Look, my mom is right over there!" He spoke to no one visible but swung an arm around behind him. "You're both here together. You're here with me, Gracie. I didn't know then, Gracie. Nothing was built, but look! You've come home!"

Nearly an hour passed before a young man and his robotic dog lifted themselves from the soft ground of the old graveyard.

"Always with me, Gracie." Theo patted his thigh. "C'mon, Murphy. We'll visit again."

Clouds of Change

"Well, Theodore, it's about time you showed up. We have an important test run on an energy capacitor today. I'll need your help aligning components with satellite power. If you don't mind, will you grab my journal of notes from the bookshelf? I need to ensure that my voice notes have been correctly transferred into cloud storage." Luke Marshall spoke with passion and even a hint of hurry in his voice.

"Sure, Dad. Uh, I know you've been studying science forever, but couldn't you do without the paper journals these days?" Theo hoped to pressure his old-fashioned dad into forgoing the pencil-and-paper journal. Not only were they an out-of-date system of recording, but it was nearly impossible to find paper for writing. Several years ago the American people were asked to limit what was written on paper to limit waste.

"Oh, probably." Luke paused while he finished waving his arms on the translucent air screen where he typed in a code. He dropped his arms to his sides. "But you know, Theo, I've learned some hard lessons in my years as a scientist. Some of the hardest lessons came from the creation and destruction by the TimeWorm. We controlled by power. We, meaning you and me. Viktor Brack, on the other hand, used power and paper and pencil."

Books, too many from decades past, lined the walls of bookshelves in Luke Marshall's office. Theo knew which section would hold the most recent journal. He reached for his father's journal of notes. Something caught his eye that made him pull back his hand. Beside his father's journal was a smooth leather book with fancy letters scrawled on the front. Theo recognized the book he had brought back from the time jump to Germany. He stared as a dizzy spinning passed behind his eyes. With a slight turn, he moved his hand to pull the book from the shelf. He ran his fingers over the etched letters—*Sociatatus*.

"Dad," Theo interrupted. "Don't you realize if Dr. Brack hadn't written his notes in this stupid journal"—he waved the leather book in the air—"I wouldn't have had to risk my life. I chased all over Nazi Germany for these notes that could have changed whether we even could stand here and have this conversation."

"True, Theo. But if we had been able to depend upon more than a single source of technology controlled by one man, maybe we wouldn't have been caught in Brack's power struggle that left me paralyzed and forced you to time jump."

"But, Dad." Theo stood straighter as if to strengthen his argument.

"No, Theo. I had a lot of time to think about all of this. I thought I had killed you by allowing the TimeWorm to break down every molecule of your being and send you over a hundred years back in time. While you were gone I blamed myself for what I had done and made promises of what I would do if I ever got you back." Luke checked his rising voice and paused to regain emotional control.

"Well, you're back. And you're right. I need to depend on technology. It's the world we've created, and it's the world we use. But I'll always have a fallback plan. Power created by man can also be controlled by man. I'll never be so dependent upon what I've written on a screen or stored in a cloud that I can't access. You know the government controls and patrols all clouds. Nothing is secret, and nothing belongs to this colony alone. All that I create and store in a cloud is reviewed by our controlling country."

"Dad, don't start getting paranoid on me. Your science is for good. Who cares what country is looking at it?" Theo tried not to sound belittling.

"I care. I care, Theo, and you should too. You time jumped into a country that stole the right of free thought and free existence from its own countrymen. We pray daily that never happens to the States of America, but we never know. Son, we never know." Luke Marshall walked to his son and put a firm hand on Theo's shoulder. "You know your past, Theo. You must be willing, if and when the need arises, to stand for what's right for your family, your people."

Theo sighed and relaxed under his father's hand. "Okay, Dad. I'll get your notes." He was proud of his father, one of the brightest scientists of the day, but he also smiled because he wanted to believe he was right.

"So here you sit, leather journal. I risked my life for you, but I can't be angry. You gave me life through my beautiful Gracie.

Theo told the stories of Germany, of *The Watch*, of Jahile, of Gracie, of her parents Grey and Lindy Cooper, of the Edelweiss Pirates over and over, and the memories still held happiness. The memories also brought pain from a still-open wound in his heart where he grieved daily. He swallowed and returned the book to the shelf.

For the next three hours, scientists Luke and Theo Marshall worked side by side programming, checking and double-checking codes, verifying current and forecast satellites, and making endless notes, both to cloud and on paper. Mutters back and forth and the soft whishing of the movement of their air chairs were finally interrupted by the momentary dissolve of the door force shield. A young woman entered.

Luke Marshall rose from his air chair in respect to the lady entering their laboratory. Theo stared and smiled at the powdery scent that floated in with the pretty young woman.

"You're just in time to help us run a test flight on this interplanetary orb!" Luke Marshall had a fresh lilt in his voice. He nearly fell, he twisted so fast to follow the eyes of the young lady. "Oh, this is my fellow scientist and, more importantly, my son, Theo." Luke made a sweeping gesture toward the smiling young man.

"Theo, meet one of the most recent employees of the Marshall Science Lab."

"Hullo." Theo stood out of reaction more than courtesy. "I'm sorry for staring, but you look very familiar."

Soft, long curls bobbed as the young female scientist smiled and nodded. "Well, if you look long enough, you may fall off your driftboard." She chuckled.

"My driftboard?" Theo knew he hadn't tried his skating skills since before his time jump five years earlier.

"Maybe if I put on my pink jogging suit you'll remember me."

"Oh, no! Huh-uh. It can't be!" Theo grinned big and shook his head. "Are you the girl who always jogged in the park where I rode my driftboard? I did every stupid stunt I could think of to get your attention, and it never worked."

"Well, my plan was to make you think I never paid attention. I was afraid if I watched you I would drift off course of finishing high school with top grades to get me into Barnard College where I could study science."

"Did you?" Theo took a step toward her while Luke grinned like a Cheshire cat.

"Did I what? Pay attention?"

"No, did you study science."

Laughing, the pretty woman picked up a lab jacket and slipped it on. "Well, here I am."

All three scientists laughed and made motion to return to the project at hand.

Work progressed for another hour until Luke Marshall set his pencil and journal on a tabletop suspended under the air screen. "Perhaps we should take a break for dinner."

Suddenly, a buzzing robotic voice came from Theo's nop. "Heart rate accelerating."

Theo grabbed his wrist computer to muffle the voice. "Thank you, IRIS. Your input is not needed at this time." His adult face held a feisty grin as he looked between his dad and the lady scientist.

"IRIS will probably tell Murphy to check your heat vision if you give her time." Luke gave a quick nod at the beagle resting at Theo's workstation.

"Dad!"

"Well, it's true. I think you've stolen more glances at our coworker than at the screen hanging in front of your face." Luke Marshall quipped and cleared a cough in his throat.

"Sorry to embarrass you with our blunt talk." Theo smiled but spoke directly to the lady whose soft skin had a caramel-toned glow. "We're just not used to having a pretty face in this lab." Theo tipped his head in the same inquisitive angle as Murphy who cocked his head at the pretty woman. "There's just something familiar about you. I'm sorry, we got so busy with work I forgot to ask your name."

"Haley." The soft curls framed her delicate face. "Haley Cooper."

Epilogue

TimeWorm Series books *TimeWorm*, *Vigilatus*, and *Rendered* not only tell the journey of a young man from the future but was itself born in the midst of life's journey.

TimeWorm, the first book of the series, originated from a young man's single notebook page of writing about a robotic dog and a boy from the future. Jimmy Adams approached colleague, friend, and soon-to-be coauthor, Brenda Heller, with the dream of writing a novel that students would enjoy as fiction and learn as history. Like the characters Theo and Gracie, the two authors began a journey that held bumps and joys that are all part of the process of writing and publishing.

The two main characters in the series were created from fiction. Many other characters reflect real names and lives of real people—both good and bad. Fictitious characters were named from people in Brenda's and Jimmy's lives, people who exemplified the strengths of the characters. Thus, the lines between fiction and reality become blurred with the hope of stirring a curiosity to know the past and to search the real events of history with the honor and horror the actual people may bring.

The series would be incomplete without the love and antics of the robotic dog. The reader may fall in love with the dog and wish he were real. In a sense, he was. The robotic dog was fashioned after Jimmy's own dog from his childhood, a beagle named Murphy, pictured here with young Jimmy.

To follow a dream is a wonderful opportunity. However, dreams are never isolated from life, and sometimes, just as in writing this series, the journey changes and one is left to carry on. During the creation of the second book, Jimmy's life took him away from the path of being an author. Though the dream still lay in his heart, time and circumstance ended his time of the journey.

A gift one traveler can give another who cannot complete a common journey is the promise of carrying through to the end. Although Jimmy could only travel for half of the journey, this shared dream has been completed by friend and coauthor, Brenda Heller.

About the Author

BRENDA HELLER WAS BORN AND raised in Middle America. Memories from her childhood recall a mother who read stories and poems with expression that whet her imagination. Years later while going through a cedar chest full of her mother's own writing, Brenda found a torn scrap of brown paper where her mother had written, "I find paper and pencil and can't help but write." Perhaps her mother passed down a passion for scripting the past into stories of the imagination.

Besides creating historical fiction, Brenda enjoys writing and teaching from the Bible. She and her husband raised two daughters and shared their lives with nine foster children. They have five grandchildren. She and her husband experience real adventure as they travel across the world and enjoy outdoor activities that take them into the wilderness and off-the-grid of society.